D1328491

THE
GREEN BOTTLE
AND THE
SILVER KITE

FREDERICKA BERGER

The
Green Bottle
and the
Silver Kite

Greenwillow Books, New York

PZ
7
B4515
Gr
1993

Copyright © 1993 by Fredericka Berger

All rights reserved. No part of this book
may be reproduced or utilized in any form
or by any means, electronic or mechanical,
including photocopying, recording, or by
any information storage and retrieval
system, without permission in writing
from the Publisher, Greenwillow Books,
a division of William Morrow & Company, Inc.,
1350 Avenue of the Americas, New York, NY 10019.

First Edition   10 9 8 7 6 5 4 3 2 1

Library of Congress Cataloging-in-Publication Data
Berger, Fredericka
The green bottle and the silver kite / by Fredericka Berger.
p.   cm.
Summary: While earning money to buy a special kite,
Phil annoys his sister and makes a new friend.
ISBN 0-688-11785-6
[1. Kites—Fiction.   2. Brothers and sisters—Fiction.
3. Beaches—Fiction.]   I. Title.
PZ7.B4515Gr   1993
[Fic]—dc20   92-10073   CIP   AC

SKIDMORE COLLEGE LIBRARY

To Conrad. And to Eric,
who once had a silver kite.

And thank you to the Hartzells.

C O N T E N T S

THE
GREEN BOTTLE
AND THE
SILVER KITE

{ It's My Turn }

The last ride had been all right, but Phil was going to make the next one even better. Although the wave had taken him fairly far in, it had ended before he got to the sandbar. An average ride, really. One in which he had felt a little bit ahead of the wave. Not altogether in harmony with it.

I'll wait longer this time, he decided as he beat his way back through the breakers, diving under the big ones while clinging to the rope around his rubber raft. When he got to the place where the breakers originated, he lay flat on the raft, waiting for the right wave. He let two negligible waves roll under him, keeping his raft sideways so he could see what was coming.

There it was. The big one. Higher and higher it rose toward him, and still he waited before he turned his raft. Now it was curving over, but it hadn't yet broken. This was the right moment. Turn. Kick. The energy of the wave surged through him, shooting him forward. He was the wave foaming in toward the shore. This time they were perfectly joined.

Was his mother looking? Could she see what a ride he was having? The bottom of the raft scraped against the sandbar. It was over too quickly. The thrill, the exhilaration gone already. Phil relaxed on the raft with his eyes closed to savor the ride for a minute longer before he went back for another.

"It's my turn," said a voice.

The raft was pulled out from under him, and he was rolled over onto the wet sand.

Maggie was too strong for a seven-year-old girl. His friends didn't have seven-year-old sisters who could pull rafts away when they were lying on them. But of course, he hadn't been on his guard. He'd been lying there like a dumb fool with his eyes closed. Maggie hadn't been on the beach when he started swimming. And he'd gotten careless.

"Hey!" Phil stood up. He had wet sand all over him. He could feel it inside his bathing suit. "You just came out on the beach. You can't have a turn yet."

"Well, how many rides have you had?" asked Maggie, starting to edge the raft out toward the surf.

"Lots," said Phil, catching the rope on the other end before she got any farther. "But they don't count. They don't start counting until you come out on the beach."

"Yes, they do," said Maggie. "They all count. If you've had ten rides, then I can have ten rides." Maggie turned and tried to pull the raft away from him.

But Phil was ten years old and, when he was on his guard, about twenty times stronger than Maggie. "We'll ask Mom," he said, pulling the other way. Ten rides! It was completely unreasonable, and Mom would tell her so and get Maggie off his back.

Or would she? Mom didn't always see things his way. And she wouldn't like being disturbed. She was sitting with two of her friends, talking while she watched him swim.

"Wait. I have an idea," said Phil. Not the best arrangement, but they could . . . "We could ride on it together," he suggested, moving back toward Maggie and letting the rope slacken.

"No," said Maggie. "You're too heavy. You make it all lopsided. I want to do it alone." She took the rope with both hands and jerked the raft away. In the spirit of compromise, Phil had relaxed his hold. The rope slipped through his fingers, and Maggie ran out toward the deeper water, the raft bumping behind her.

Phil knew she wouldn't go far. She liked catching the waves once they'd broken. He ran after her and lunged for the rope. Splash! Into the shallow water. Had he got it?

Yes. No. A wave washed over him. As Maggie pulled away again, he groped wildly through the water. Yes, got it. So much for you, Maggie. He stood up and pulled. Maggie held on, and Phil pulled, back across the sandbar, up the slope of the beach, dragging the raft and Maggie behind him.

Halfway along Maggie dropped to her knees, a dead weight in the sand. But she didn't let go of the rope. There was no way he could keep on pulling Maggie and the raft up the steep slope.

"Let go," Phil threatened. "Or I'll get it away from you if it's the last thing I—"

"No, you won't," said Maggie. "I'll never let go."

"All right," said Phil. He lifted the raft and started to turn it so that the rope on Maggie's end twisted tighter and tighter around her fingers.

"Let go," he warned as he turned.

"No," said Maggie. But the next minute she was screaming, "Ow! Ow! Mom, ouch! Help!"

"Let go," said Phil. Why didn't that stupid kid let go? He really didn't want to hurt her. He might even let her have the raft for one ride on condition that she'd take the ride after that with him. He'd much rather be playing with her than fighting with her.

"What's the problem?" Phil heard his mother's voice behind him.

"It's my turn," said Maggie.

"She pulled it right out from under me," said Phil. "Without asking." But he didn't feel like struggling anymore.

"And is it her turn?"

"I guess so," said Phil wearily.

"You should have asked first, Maggie," Mom scolded. Maggie was already maneuvering the raft back into the water. She'd probably keep it for ten rides unless he made a fuss.

Phil went to get his towel. He took it far away from everyone else and spread it out. There was no one to play with. Albert was over by the bay fishing from the dock. He'd invited Phil to come along. But Phil thought fishing was too dull. He lay on his towel looking at the sky. Nothing could be duller than this, he thought. Maybe I should go find Albert.

It wasn't long before Maggie brought the raft back to him. Out of the corner of his eye he saw her drop it on the sand. "You can have it now," she said.

Phil sat up and looked out at the ocean. The tide had changed, and the waves were breaking farther in. Riding waves wouldn't be as much fun now.

"Want to play Frisbee?" he asked.

"No," said Maggie. "I'm going inside."

"What for? It's nicer out here."

"I'm going to play with your old Matchbox toys."

"Bring them out on the beach."

"No."

"Oh, come on, Maggie. Why not?"

"They'll get sandy."

"They're my Matchbox toys, and I don't mind if they get sandy," said Phil.

"Well, I do," said Maggie.

Phil lay back on his towel and closed his eyes. When he opened them, Maggie was gone. He wished he'd held on to her pigtail and made her stay. He closed his eyes again. He could hear his mother talking with her friends. One of them was Albert's mother. But he couldn't hear what they were saying.

"*Boop, boop.*" That was Albert's little sister pushing her red plastic boat around in the sand. Three years old. She was too young to be of any use to anybody.

Then he heard a very strange sound. "*Whiffle, whiffle, whiffle.*" It got closer. "*Whiffle, whiffle.*" It got farther away. "*Whiffle, whiffle, whiffle.*" It was right on top of him. It was landing on him. Shielding his forehead with his arm as though to protect himself, Phil opened his eyes. Where did it come from? He couldn't see. But he still heard the noise. Fainter now. "*Whiffle, whiffle.*" He looked up higher and saw in the sky above him a silver bird mounting farther and farther toward the clouds. Suddenly it plunged back, then just as suddenly climbed higher again. Phil could almost believe it was alive. But it strained at something. A string. That's what it must be.

"*Whiffle, whiffle,*" it called as it shivered in the wind.

I wish I were a kite, Phil thought. I could be up high and pretend to dive down on people and frighten them.

"*Boop, boop.*" Albert's little sister pushed her boat under Phil's knees as though they were a bridge.

"Get away," said Phil. He wanted to keep on imagining he was a kite.

I'd dive down on Maggie and Albert and possibly Albert's little sister. Although she doesn't really matter. And then I'd go back up in the sky again and be free of them all, he thought.

"Seeing lions in the clouds, Phillie?" His mother was

standing near him, holding her chair and beach bag. He was a kite. He couldn't answer. But she didn't wait. "Don't forget the raft," she called out as she started toward the house. Then Albert's mother came and got his little sister before she had time to make another passage under Phil's legs.

The raft. Caught. Maggie had left the raft for him to carry in. Well, he wouldn't do it. If he were a kite, he couldn't carry rafts. "Maggie used it last," he called after his mother. But she didn't hear him.

How could he manage not to carry the raft back to the house? Maggie should have done it.

He looked upward again, searching out the kite. It was right above him—sinking closer and moving away as though it were beckoning to him. I'll play with you, it seemed to say. A kite for a playmate. It wouldn't go fishing. And it wouldn't be entitled to a turn on the raft. And if it were his kite . . . ("It's Phil's kite," he could hear Mom telling Maggie. "Leave it alone.") If it were his kite, he wouldn't have to share it with anyone else. If only he owned a kite like that, a silver kite.

{ The Bat Kite Smiled }

"Can I come with you?" Phil asked his mother the next morning when she said she was going shopping.

"For what?" asked Maggie. She was lying on her stomach on the living room floor, lining up the Matchbox toys in their "garage" under the wicker couch.

"A kite," said Phil.

"Didn't we have one last year?" Maggie asked. "Remember? Aunt Brenda brought it in her suitcase."

"It didn't fly very well," said Phil, "even after we put a tail on it."

"I remember," said Mom. "It landed on Bertram's roof, and we couldn't get it down."

"And it wasn't my kite," said Phil. "It was everybody's."

"I don't even want a kite," said Maggie, turning over on her back and kicking her legs in the air.

"So what?" said Phil. "I do."

His mother was looking in her purse for her car keys. "I think you'd better come, too, Maggie," she said.

"Albert might bring his little sister over."

"Then call and tell them to come this afternoon."

"But she'll be disappointed," Maggie complained. "Why can't you shop this afternoon?"

"What about me?" said Phil. "I'm more important than Albert's little sister."

"Come on, you two," said Phil's mother, rumpling his hair, making him feel good. She pulled Maggie up to a standing position and pushed her toward the telephone. "If I don't go shopping this morning, you won't have any lunch."

Before they left, Maggie insisted on finding her visor. It was an old tennis visor, dirty and spotted with rust. Maggie never went shopping without it. Weird. That was the only way to describe her appearance. It embarrassed Phil. Visor sticking out one way and pigtail sticking out the other. Strangers in the stores made jokes about it. Even so, Phil was glad she would be there to see him buy the silver kite.

"How much does a kite cost?" Phil asked his mother as they drove north on Ocean Avenue.

"Oh, a couple of dollars," she said. "You brought your money along?"

Phil felt in his pocket. Where was it? Maybe the other pocket. Not there either. His camper shorts had too many pockets. Now he remembered. He had put his money in the one with the zipper.

"Here it is. A dollar and"—he dug down farther—"four quarters."

"Should be enough," said Mom, turning left away from the beach into the shopping section of Point Pleasant.

"Groceries first," she said, "and then we'll look for the kite." Phil surveyed the two rows of shops along the main street of Point Pleasant. In which one would they find his silver kite? The five-and-ten? The hobby shop? The drug-store that sold toys?

What about Maggie? Would she last while they went from store to store? She didn't complain when she got tired. But she drooped quietly and dramatically in a way that always shortened a shopping trip.

As it was, after the drugstore and the five-and-ten she went back to the car. Phil and his mother persevered.

"I thought you meant a paper kite," Mom said as they walked along the hot pavement. "That's what we always had when we were children."

"Aunt Brenda's was plastic," said Phil.

"Well, plastic then. But you didn't like the plastic one in the drugstore, and it cost a dollar ninety-eight."

"Aunt Brenda's was plastic. Mine is silver." It was like trying to explain a dream. "Mine." Phil had said "mine" as though he possessed the kite. Maybe there was only one silver kite in the world, and that already belonged to someone else. The hobby shop was his last hope. It had the most complete collection of Matchbox toys in Ocean County. Why not kites?

His mother was getting tired. As soon as they got in the door, she asked the boy at the cash register, "Do you sell kites?"

Of course, they did. Phil could have told her that.

"Yeah," said the boy, "over there." He pointed to a box that had thin sticks, the ends of rolled-up kites, poking out of it.

"Do you sell silver kites?"

Wasn't Mom going to go over and look? The kid at the cash register might not know what kinds of kites were in the box.

"I've never seen one," the kid was saying as Phil pulled his mother over to the kites.

"Let's check, Mom," Phil insisted.

His mother helped him pull out each kite in the box. Most were plastic. A few were paper. Phil checked the last one. It was stuck over in a corner of the box in a way that suggested it was different from the other kites. Phil closed his eyes and reached for it. This will be the silver one, he promised himself. He opened his eyes. The kite sticks were wrapped with red and yellow plastic.

"I guess that's it, Phillie," Mom said. "At least for Point Pleasant. I can't think of any other stores that might sell kites. Are you sure you don't want the plastic kite? It's very pretty."

Phil didn't waste his breath answering. Instead he dropped the plastic kite back in the box. There must be other places in the world where one might hope to find a silver kite. But how far away were they and how long would it take to get there? Would he have to go all the way to China?

"You can ask my mother," said a voice from behind the cash register. "She's in the back room."

"Since we're here," said Mom with a sigh, "I guess we might as well."

The woman in the back room was sitting at a desk piled with papers and catalogs. She was writing and talking on the telephone at the same time.

"Maybe she can order one," Phil's mother whispered while they waited for her to finish the conversation.

How long would that take? Phil wanted the silver kite right away.

"A silver kite?" said the woman. "That's a specialty item. We wouldn't carry anything like that. I guess you've tried the kite store."

The kite store! If such a place existed, it was surely the place to find a silver kite.

"Just over the bridge in Manasquan," said the woman. "First right, and three traffic lights . . ."

Phil didn't hear the rest. His mother could worry about that. He only heard the *"whiffle, whiffle"* of the silver kite.

When Mom told Maggie they were driving over the inlet to Manasquan, she moaned, threw herself back against the seat, and pulled her visor down over her face. For a moment Phil thought his mother would decide to take Maggie home. But she turned north toward the inlet, saying, "I promise. This will be the last stop."

It was a small store, wedged between a cleaner's and an automobile supply shop. They would have missed it if there hadn't been kites hanging outside. A round sau-cer-shaped kite with a silver tail. A long red snaky kite. Even though it was small, it looked like a store that had every kind of kite imaginable. Phil put his fingers against his pocket. He could feel the money there ready to be spent.

It wasn't a question of whether the store had the silver kite, Phil realized as soon as they got inside, but of whether it could be found in the jumble of kites hanging from every possible surface.

I'll find it for sure, Phil thought. If only they give me enough time.

Maggie had come in with them and was reaching toward a butterfly-shaped kite.

"Don't touch," Mom reminded her.

"I know," said Maggie. "Do you see your kite?" she asked Phil.

"No, but I will in a minute," he said, warding off Mag-gie's impatience. And he did. It was hanging over the door. A silver kite in the shape of a shield with a red dragon on it. Did the one he'd seen on the beach have a dragon? It must have, because Phil knew this was the kite.

"There it is, Mom," said Phil, pointing.

"It's very pretty." She'd said the same thing about the plastic kite. "But . . ." Something seemed to be worrying her. "Let's find out," was all she said. "Hello," she called. There didn't appear to be anyone else in the store.

"May I help you?" A man came out from behind a screen of kites at the far end. He looked like a kite himself, a bat kite, with his dark-rimmed glasses and his hair sticking straight out on either side of his head.

"We're interested in that kite," said Mom, indicating the kite over the door. "Right, Phil?"

The bat kite smiled. "That's a very good choice," he said. "For you?" He nodded toward Phil.

"Yes," said Phil.

"It's well balanced, scientifically designed, and—"

"How much does it cost?" asked Mom.

"It's made of Mylar," the man continued.

"What's Mylar?" asked Phil.

"It's used in weather balloons," said the man, "and suits for astronauts."

"And how much does it cost?" repeated Phil's mother.

Phil had his pocket unzipped, ready to yield the money.

"That kite," said the man, "is a good buy at fourteen dollars and ninety-five cents."

Silence. Mom looked over at Phil, then back at the bat kite man. "We'll have to think about it," she said, and they left. "I knew it," she said after they got into the car, "when I didn't see any prices. And in a little store like that. They don't sell a lot, so it's always expensive."

Phil didn't say anything. Maggie sat in back with her chin on the front seat, looking at him from under her visor. Phil didn't care. He didn't even bother to remind her to put her seat belt on.

"We just bought the raft, Phil." Mom seemed disappointed, too. "We can't buy another expensive thing for you right away."

"That was for both of us," said Phil. "That wasn't mine."

"Well . . . If we bought it, you'd have to share it, of course."

"I wanted to buy it myself," said Phil. "I wanted to

get it today." He wished that he hadn't found the silver kite. Or did he? Wasn't it better at least to know it was there?

"We'll sit down and talk about finances when your father gets home tonight," said Mom, patting his knee.

Finances? Tonight? So much money. Such a long time to wait. Phil could feel Maggie's visor poking his shoulder, but he didn't protest. When he got back to the house, he went inside right away without looking up into the sky where he might have seen the silver kite.

{ Definitely Something }

"What time is it?" Phil asked.

Albert turned his arm carefully so as not to jiggle his fishing rod and looked at his waterproof, shockproof, self-winding watch. Lots of people had watches like that, thought Phil, but not many had silver kites.

"Three-twelve and thirty-six seconds," said Albert. He was precise about everything. Maybe that was why he caught so many fish. He was precise and patient. He threaded the bait slowly so that it ran up the length of the hook and concealed it completely. Then he made a short cast into the water and waited. No pulling the line in to see if there was still bait on the hook.

Three o'clock. Three hours to wait until his father got back from New York and they could discuss finances. Albert might be good at waiting, but Phil wasn't. He reeled his line in. The bait was hanging loosely, but at least it was still there. He cast it back impatiently and crossed Albert's line.

"Watch it," said Albert. "Wait a minute. Lift your rod over my head and . . ." With Albert's placid guidance, Phil separated his line and cast it again farther down the bulkhead. But as soon as he got it in, he decided he was bored with fishing. Three hours would be like three years if he spent it fishing.

He'd go home and see if he could amuse himself with Maggie and Albert's little sister. He'd even pretend to play with their dolls if they'd let him. Soon, maybe tomorrow. It depended on the talk about finances. Soon he could forget about fishing and dolls. He'd be busy flying his silver kite.

Four dolls covered with a beach towel lay on the wicker couch. Only their heads were showing.

"Maggie," Phil called. "Mom." No answer. They must be on the beach. He ran out the porch door to the top of the sand dune and stopped. If he wasn't careful not to look up, he'd see the silver kite. And he didn't want to. Not until he had one of his own.

He came down the sand dune, looking straight toward his mother seated in her beach chair, talking with her friends. Maggie was nearby, kneeling in the sand behind Albert's little sister, pointing up into the sky.

"See it?" she was saying as Phil came up. "Oh, Phil, is that the kite?"

"Guess so," said Phil. He looked at Albert's little sister's feet. "You don't need to tell everyone in the world about it," he muttered.

Albert's little sister had short, fat feet, and one of them was standing on a black Frisbee, bending it in the middle.

"Hey, that's my Frisbee," said Phil.

"It isn't," said Maggie. "The ocean washed it in."

"Well, I got it out of the ocean," said Phil.

"Well, I saw it first," said Maggie.

Albert's little sister picked up the Frisbee and jerked it toward Phil.

"Look out!" said Phil, leaping aside before it hit him in the teeth. It wobbled down into the sand behind him, and he ran to pick it up.

"Give it to me, Phil," said Maggie. "I'm going to teach her to play Frisbee."

"You don't know how to do it right," said Phil.

"Come on, Phil," Maggie begged. "You can play, too."

With Albert's little sister, who came up only to his knees? Who couldn't catch a big rubber ball when you threw it right at her from two feet away? That would be a joke.

"All right," said Phil to Albert's little sister, pretending to take it all seriously. "All right. Are you ready?" He took his arm back with an exaggerated sweep and brought it forward with a flourish. He let the Frisbee fly out of his grasp in a high, wide arc. What a throw it was! What a joke it all was, playing Frisbee with a three-year-old.

What a throw indeed! It went high into the air toward the ocean, flattened out over the sandbar, and slid down onto the still water beyond the breakers. It landed too far away for a wave to carry it back in and too far away for Phil to swim out and get it.

"It's your fault," said Phil.

"Mine?" said Maggie, standing up and kicking a little sand at him.

"You brought it out," said Phil, kicking more sand back. Some of it spattered on Albert's little sister, and she started to cry.

"*Wa-a-a-a-h!*" She ran over to where the mothers were sitting. Albert's mother turned and put an arm around her and wiped her face with a towel. Phil could hear her whimpering and talking, but he couldn't hear what she was saying.

"Phil." Mom stood up and walked over to them. "Maggie. What's the problem?"

Maggie and Phil exchanged a quick look of agreement. Forget the sand, it said. And the question of who was at fault. Rescue the Frisbee, it said.

"We've lost the Frisbee," Phil said. And Maggie nodded and pointed out toward the ocean.

They all three stood at the edge of the water and looked.

"See it?" said Phil.

"No," said Mom.

"Right there," said Maggie, pointing again.

Mom looked for a minute. Then she said, "I think I can see it."

"Could I go out on the raft and get it, Mom?" Phil asked.

"No, it's too far," she said. "If it's where I think it is."

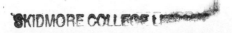
SKIDMORE COLLEGE L

"Why not, Mom?" argued Maggie. "Phil's a good swimmer."

"Can I, Mom?" Phil ran to get the raft. For once Maggie was right. She was talking the way a younger sister should talk. He hurried back, carrying it, almost tripping over the pull rope, which dragged in the sand.

"I'll take it," said Mom.

"Oh, Mom," said Phil.

"It's too far." She was firm. "If you fell off the raft, you'd have a long way to swim without any waves to help." Before he could protest further, she was in the water, pulling the raft behind her.

While he and Maggie went out on the sandbar and pointed, Mom lay on the raft, paddling around beyond the breakers, looking for the Frisbee in vain. Every ripple in the water started to look like a black Frisbee. So Phil and Maggie gave up pointing. Mom shook her head in defeat and caught a rider that landed her almost at their feet. She stood up laughing with the excitement of the ride, pushing back her wet hair. Then she looked serious.

"Sorry, dears," she said. What a great mother, jumping into the water even though she didn't like to get wet till later in the afternoon.

"Thanks for trying," said Phil. "It was our best Frisbee." That's the way it seemed, now that it was gone. "If Maggie hadn't . . ." But there was no point in getting started on that.

Phil walked away down the beach, kicking through the shallow water, idly hoping to find the Frisbee. The tide was coming in. Maybe the Frisbee had washed close to shore farther along. He rather hoped someone would follow or call to him, but no one did. When he looked back, he saw his mother sitting down again with Maggie next to her holding Albert's little sister on her lap.

What time was it? How long still before the talk about finances? And would the talk bring him the silver kite as easily as the waves had brought the Frisbee when it first washed ashore? He looked toward the foaming surf for an answer. Was that the Frisbee now, being returned by the helpful waves? Phil stopped and looked carefully. Something black was bouncing about in the wave that was nearing the sandbar. Phil ran through the shallow water to catch it before it tumbled out of sight.

It was something. It was definitely something. He grabbed for it. The wave carried it past him. He ran after the wave and grabbed again, blindly. Got it! What luck! It was hard and slippery and long. It wasn't the Frisbee; it was . . . Phil pulled it out of the water. A green bottle.

Phooey. Phil almost threw it back in. But he decided it was better than not finding anything. He held it up to the light and looked at the green, misshapen houses through it. Then he started back along the beach, swinging it as he walked.

Maggie ran to meet him. "Oh, I thought it was the Frisbee," she said, looking down at the bottle.

"What time is it?" Phil asked.

"How would I know?" she said. "You aren't going to keep it, are you?"

"Of course I am," said Phil.

"What for?" said Maggie, trying to catch it as Phil swung it back and forth.

"Well . . ." said Phil. He held the bottle up and looked

at it. Why would he keep it? It wasn't beautiful or rare. What use might it have? He noticed that the bottle was dry. It had a cork at the top. You could put something in it and it wouldn't get wet.

"Why would you want to keep it?" persisted Maggie.

"To put a note in, what else?"

Phil ran up to the house with the bottle under his arm. First he went to the kitchen to find out what time it was. Four-thirty. Then he went upstairs slowly, trying to make each step last for twenty minutes, and put the green bottle on his bureau. Then he sat on his bed and looked out. He hadn't meant to see it, but he did. Almost outside his window. The silver kite straining toward him as though it were a friend asking him to come and play.

{ Money }

"Sounds like an expensive kite," said Phil's father. They were eating dessert, Phil and his mother and father, while Maggie, who didn't like blueberries, was putting the plates in the dishwasher.

"Not for a Mylar kite," said Phil.

"That's interesting," said his father. "Mylar. They use it for weather balloons. Because it's light and strong. Should work well in a kite."

"One that's scientifically designed," said Phil, popping a blueberry into his mouth.

"Well, maybe it is worth fifteen dollars." Phil's father frowned and nodded his head the way he did when he was telling a friend to "buy gold." "How much cash have you got?" he asked Phil.

"You mean, to pay for the kite?" said Phil. He could see Maggie peeking at the kitchen door, holding a plate in each hand.

"Right," said his father. "If you were paying for it tomorrow, how much money would you have?" he explained.

"Two dollars and twenty-five cents," said Phil, sliding forward in his chair. "I do have the twenty-five-dollar savings bond that my grandfather gave me," he added, "but it's at home."

"And it's capital," said his father. "Never touch capital unless you have to."

"Well, I have to," said Phil, "or I won't have enough money."

"I mean an emergency, like illness," his father explained.

"What about a loan?" suggested Mom.

There was a crash in the kitchen. They all waited to hear what noise would come next.

"It's okay," Maggie called out. "They landed in the dishwasher."

"You know how I feel about loans, dear," said Phil's father. "Our whole society is—"

"But then Phil could get the kite now, and he could enjoy it for the rest of the summer." Phil's mother reached for his empty blueberry saucer and piled it on her own as she talked. She smiled sympathetically at Phil.

"There's a way," said Phil's father, putting both hands flat down on the table, "and it wouldn't take too long. And when Phil went to buy the kite, he'd have his own money in his pocket."

Maggie came and sat down by Phil as though she were part of the discussion when it was none of her business.

"You can take these out now," said Mom, handing the dessert dishes to Maggie. She carried them out to the kitchen walking backward.

"Phil could earn the money," Dad said just as Maggie disappeared slowly through the kitchen door.

"Earn the money?" said Phil. "Earn it?" He thought of the lemonade stand Maggie set up with Albert's little sister on hot days when the traffic was backed up. Was that what his father meant. "Earn it?" he said a third time. "How?"

"You could work," Dad said. Phil's father and mother waited and looked at Phil while Phil thought about work.

The word had an unpleasant sound. It sounded like a karate chop—the kind that breaks boards in half. Work. He couldn't think of anything good about work. It was something one had to do. If one didn't do it, one got into trouble. Schoolwork—reading, spelling, numbers. Housework— making beds, sweeping sand off stairs, loading the dishwasher. Work was unpleasant, and the only reason people ever did it was that something more unpleasant happened to them if they didn't.

"I'm doing enough work," he protested. "This is my vacation."

"We'd pay you a dollar fifty an hour for real work," Dad urged.

It sounded as though it would take a lot of hours to make

$14.95. Dad might as well have said "work for the rest of the summer." One extra hour of work during vacation was too much.

"No," said Phil. "No, I don't want to."

"I'm sorry," said his father. "Work can be fun. And there's plenty here that needs to be done. And then you'd have the kite."

"I don't want to work," said Phil. "I don't care that much about the kite."

"But it would be a good idea, Phil," said Mom. "Your father's right. You'd feel better about it if you earned the money."

"Let me know," said Dad, getting up from the table, "if you change your mind."

"I'd rather go to Atlantic City and gamble," Phil called after him. His father didn't answer.

"Oh, Phillie," said Mom, laughing as she left the table.

Phil stayed where he was while Mom wiped the place mats and put them away. She looked at him, but she didn't say anything.

"Whatcha thinking?" Maggie was at his elbow.

"Money," Phil whispered. "And how to get it quickly. Without working."

"What about Monopoly?" Maggie suggested.

Phil hooted. "That's only pretend money."

"I mean, playing," said Maggie.

They spread the set out on the fuzzy rug and sat down cross-legged to play.

"I'll be the banker," said Phil. If only this money, all this money, were real. And if it were mine, he thought, as he distributed the fifties, the hundreds, and the five-hundred-dollar notes.

"You owe me one hundred dollars' rent," said Maggie. It hadn't taken her long to acquire Boardwalk and Park Place. Soon there'd be houses and then a hotel. Phil didn't want to stay around and go bankrupt.

"I'm sleepy." He yawned and stretched, knocking the board so that the pieces slid out of place. His own house on Baltic Avenue slipped over to Community Chest.

"Look how you've messed it up," said Maggie.

"I'm going to bed," said Phil.

"Sore loser," Maggie called after him as he started toward the stairs.

"It's still early, dear." Mom looked at him questioningly. Dad looked up from the newspaper.

"I'm going to think," said Phil with his hand on the banister. "I'm going to think about something I can do." They waited. "Like—like renting something." There was a pause. Nobody said anything. Phil started upstairs.

"Good night," his parents called after him.

"Phil's got to help clear up," he heard Maggie saying.

He kept on going. He went into his room and closed the door.

But I don't have anything to rent, he thought, looking out at the moonlit beach, no houses or hotels. He could rent his Matchbox toys to Maggie, except that she'd spent all her money on a tea set for her dolls.

Phil got his pajamas on in the dark and climbed into bed. The moonlight was so bright he had trouble going to sleep. He kept feeling he should do something about it. From his window he could see the path it made on the ocean.

Follow, the silent moonlight seemed to say. Follow the path.

Where would it lead? Phil wondered.

To what you long for.

To the silver kite. If only he could follow the path, if he could walk on the water. It would take a miracle to get the kite.

A miracle, he thought sleepily. Where would he find one? He looked around his room. His books, his airplanes, his three-masted schooner—they all had an alert look, as if they were ready to come alive and help him. Then he saw the green bottle on his bureau with the moonlight glowing through it. A miracle, he thought, and fell asleep.

CHAPTER 5

{ Good Luck }

"If I put a note in the bottle and threw it in the ocean and got an answer, that would be a miracle," Phil said to himself when he woke up the next morning. The idea was in his head waiting for him as though his brain had been busy thinking it up while he was asleep.

He went over to his bureau and picked up the green bottle. Then he held it toward the morning sunlight, which was slanting across the sand dune into his window. It was important to be completely sure that there wasn't a drop of water in it. He turned it upside down. Nothing ran along the side. The green glass still looked clear and dry.

With the bottle in one hand, he tiptoed over and opened the door with the other. He looked up and down the hall. All the doors were closed. He listened. No sound of footsteps or people getting dressed. It must be early still. And it was Saturday morning, so his parents would be sleeping late. That was good because what he wanted to do needed to be done in secret.

Why? Because otherwise it wouldn't work, he told himself as he tiptoed downstairs, still in his pajamas. Why? He asked himself again. But there wasn't time to answer that question. He was already in the kitchen, opening the drawer of large spoons and forks and odds and ends, hoping to find something he could use to get the cork out of the bottle.

It was a noisy drawer full of metal things that rattled against one another when he pulled it open. He stopped like a robber afraid of being caught. No noise from above. Then he inched it out the rest of the way and canvassed the contents. A wooden potato masher, a whetstone for sharpening knives, pincers for picking up live crabs, an ice pick. Clearly that would push the cork into the bottle rather than get it out.

As though he were playing pick-up-sticks, Phil reached through the maze of ladles and forks for the corkscrew. Got it! Without a sound. But was it what he wanted? He turned it around, considering whether he would be able to use it without crumbling the cork. The cork did stick out a little bit beyond the bottle. Maybe . . .

"Whatcha doing?"

Phil jumped. But he only did it inside. Otherwise he would surely have dropped the bottle.

"Maggie! What are you doing up so early?"

"Are you sending a note?" Maggie asked, pointing to the bottle.

Phil couldn't keep anything secret from Maggie. But maybe it didn't matter if Maggie knew he was sending a note as long as she didn't know what was in the note. She looked harmless enough with her blond hair loose on her shoulders and her bare feet sticking out from under her seashell nightgown.

"Yes, I am," said Phil.

"What about?" asked Maggie.

"None of your business," said Phil. "And don't tell Mom and Dad. Promise."

No answer.

"Promise, Maggie. You've got to."

"If you'll let me help," said Maggie.

"Well . . ." said Phil. "Say you promise." He waved the bottle threateningly at her.

"I promise," said Maggie, jerking her head forward for emphasis.

"Good," said Phil. "Now, if you hold the bottle . . . And I take these pliers . . ." He got them out of the drawer, not worrying quite as much about the noise. "Now hold, Maggie, with both hands."

Phil pulled at the bit of cork that was sticking out of the bottle. The bottle and Maggie both tipped forward. That wasn't going to work.

"Brace yourself, Maggie," Phil instructed. "See?" He showed her how to put one foot behind the other and bend her knees. Phil pulled, and Maggie braced.

"I can't hold any longer," Maggie complained.

"One more minute," Phil said. "It's coming. It's almost—"

Pop! Maggie fell back against the kitchen stool, still holding the bottle, while Phil clutched the cork with the pliers. Neither of them moved or said a word.

The bottle was in one piece! Maggie was clasping it to her with both hands. She was a good accomplice, thought Phil, even though she had fallen down. She hadn't let out a squeal and hadn't dropped the bottle.

A door opened upstairs. Someone came down the hall. "What's going on?" said a deep, sleepy voice.

Phil tried to think of a truthful and uncomplicated answer. "Maggie fell," he called back.

"If you children can't be quiet," the voice continued, "go out on the beach and play." Then they heard footsteps moving along the hall. A door closed.

Whew! thought Phil. Almost discovered.

"Have you got the note?" asked Maggie, sitting more comfortably on the floor with her legs in front of her.

"I'll be right back," said Phil. "Wait here. Promise." He didn't want Maggie looking over his shoulder while he wrote it.

"I promise," Maggie said.

Phil took a sheet of paper from his mother's shopping list tablet and a ballpoint pen and went into the dining room. He sat at the table and wrote quickly so as to finish before Maggie got tired of waiting.

To you if you find this bottle.
I need $14.95.
Please send it right away to . . .

And he wrote his address: "Box 107, Squan Beach, New Jersey."

He stood and read it over the way his teachers were always telling him to. It said everything that needed to be said, except . . . Phil turned back and wrote, "Thank you, Phillip G.," at the end. Then he hurried to the kitchen.

Maggie leaped toward him like an uncoiled spring. "Here." She held the bottle in front of his nose.

Phil rolled the paper up before Maggie could look at it, took the bottle from her, and slipped it in. With much twisting and pushing, he got the cork back into the top with the same little bit sticking out as before.

While he struggled with the cork, Maggie disappeared into the living room. Phil could hear her murmuring to the Matchbox toys, "Now you go first, and then you go, and you're the smallest, so you go last."

He held the bottle out at arm's length to get an impression of how it would look if he had found it on the beach. "Maggie." He went in to show it to her. "Doesn't it look just the way it should?"

"Now you go here, and you go over there." Maggie was still talking to the Matchbox toys. She seemed to have lost interest in the bottle.

All right, Phil decided. I'll throw it in by myself. When he came back through the living room after getting his shorts and shirt on, Maggie was gone and the door to the beach was unlocked. He found her standing down near the ocean. The sun was shining through her nightgown in a way that made her look almost naked.

"Maggie," said Phil, "you can't come out on the beach like that."

"I thought you wanted me to be quiet," said Maggie.

"If Mom sees you . . ."

Phil looked down at the bottle to admire it one last time. "Good luck," he whispered to it as though it were a soldier being sent on a dangerous mission. Then he lifted it above his head.

"Can you throw it far enough?" Maggie asked. What a question! He only had to get it past the breakers, and since it was high tide, and the breakers were close to shore, he thought he wouldn't have much trouble.

"Of course I can," said Phil, stretching his arm way back and bringing it forward with all the force he could muster. The bottle flew out of his grasp straight into the white, bubbling center of a wave that had just broken. Bottles didn't soar as easily as Frisbees.

"It's going to wash back in," said Maggie.

"I know," said Phil. He didn't need her to tell him.

As the wave carried the bottle up the slope toward them, Phil and Maggie both ran forward to catch it. Maggie got to it first. The water splashed up onto her nightgown so that the wet spots stuck to her. The color of her skin showed through, making her look even more naked than before.

"You'd better change," said Phil, taking the bottle from her, "or you'll be in trouble."

"I want to watch it go out to sea," Maggie insisted.

The thought worried Phil. Suppose the bottle went

straight across the ocean to Spain. How long would it take? And would anyone be able to read his note once the bottle got there?

This time Phil threw the bottle in a higher arc that he hoped would end far enough out.

"It's—it's . . ." said Maggie as they both shaded their eyes to watch. "Not going to make it," she finished when the bottle landed in a wave that was just curling over to break—the perfect moment to catch a rider.

Phil didn't say anything. But he made sure he was the one who got the bottle this time when it washed back in. The muscles in his arm were already tense with his determination to get it out beyond the breakers.

"I'll be back later," said Maggie. "I'm going to change."

"You'll be too late then," said Phil. This time he swung his arm around and around and finally let the bottle fly forward. It landed like a dud firecracker at the edge of the waves.

Phil lost count of how many times he picked up and threw the bottle. Maggie didn't come back. She couldn't have helped, but she was company.

"Breakfast time, Phil." His father was suddenly standing beside him.

"Okay," said Phil. The bottle was just washing in—again. Phil ignored it for a minute, letting the ocean carry it back and forth along the slope. He hoped Dad would leave before he had to rescue it. And in that moment, with Dad standing next to him, it came to him quite clearly why the note in the bottle had to be secret. His father would think it was begging, and he would disapprove. Even more than he disapproved of a loan.

A wave washed the bottle up again, almost to their feet, and left it lying in front of them on the wet sand. It was impossible to ignore. Phil's father picked it up. "Shall we throw this back in?" he asked, swinging it at his side.

What had Maggie told him? Anything? Everything? Phil was paralyzed. He couldn't answer.

"Think we can get it to Spain?" Dad lifted the bottle above his head and threw. The bottle glided almost like the black Frisbee beyond the farthest breaker. Then he brushed the wet sand off his hands. "Let's go," he said. "Your mom's cooking waffles."

As Phil followed him back up the beach, he didn't even dare say "Thank you."

CHAPTER 6

{ It's Up to You }

"I'll get the mail," said Phil after Maggie had left the breakfast table. He was afraid to talk about the mail in front of her. He was afraid she'd start asking about the note in the bottle. As it was, Mom looked at him questioningly.

"Again?" she said. "It is a big help. Want another waffle first?"

"No, thanks," said Phil.

The waffles didn't taste as good as they had last Saturday after the launching of the bottle. Since then there had been five morning visits to a mailbox that contained letters for Mom and Dad and a postcard for him from a school friend, but no answer to the message in the bottle. If he waited much longer, the summer would be over and he would never have flown the silver kite.

"I guess I'll go now." Phil got up from the table. He put his dishes in the dishwasher and went back through the living room. Maggie was lying on her stomach in the center of the living room floor, waiting for Albert's little sister to come over. Phil put his bare foot flat on her back.

"Ouch!" screamed Maggie.

"It doesn't hurt yet," he said, stepping over her instead.

Maggie sat up. "Have you gotten an answer?" she asked.

"No," said Phil. "And even if I had, I wouldn't tell anyone." He let the screen door slam behind him. All Maggie ever did was play with Matchbox toys and Albert's little sister and ask him whether he'd gotten an answer.

Phil believed he would get one that day. It was the kind of day when good things ought to happen. The sun was shining, and there was a cool breeze from the ocean. If the money came today, would Mom be willing to drive him immediately up to Manasquan for the kite? He hadn't thought out how he was going to explain the money to his parents once he received it. The prospect made him uncomfortable. As he got closer to the post office, he almost started to hope the money wasn't there.

B right to J. Twice around and back to D. Phil turned the combination dial on the postbox. He took out what ap-

peared to be a thick pile of letters. Advertising from a su-
permarket in Brick Town. He dropped it in the trash. Two
letters—personal letters, not bills. One for Mom. And
one— When he saw his name on the envelope, Phil almost
dropped the pile of mail. Phillip Grant. He read it again to
be sure. Phil-lip-Grant.

He put all the other mail down on the counter and felt
the envelope, bending it back and forth. Was there money
inside? It wasn't very thick. No. Phil shook his head. No
round, bulging coins to be felt. But money. Paper money.
Was there any? Phil stopped worrying about what he
would tell his parents. What they would think. He remembered the silver kite and hoped, hoped there was money in
the envelope.

People brushed past him on their way to the window to
buy stamps or collect packages. He wouldn't open the letter
where all the world could see.

As though he had just received a secret message or stolen
goods, he sneaked out of the post office and turned away
from the ocean toward the yacht club. He'd go out to the
very end of the long dock, past the sailors, who would be
too busy with their boats to notice him, and open the letter
there.

But as he crossed the street, a disturbing thought oc-
curred to him. The letter was addressed to Phillip Grant.
He had signed the note in the bottle "Phillip G." Who
then? Who was this person who knew his last name? Someone who knew who he was, who would tell his parents,
had found the bottle! He tore open the envelope. Only a
letter. One sheet. No money hidden inside. And it was

signed . . . He stood glued to the melting macadam, perspiring drops of disappointment and relief. "Aunt Brenda." From somewhere in California. Of course, she always wrote when she traveled. Letters he usually loved to get, even though Mom made him answer them. But this time. What a scare!

Phil scrunched the letter back in the envelope. He unstuck his sneakers and continued across the street toward the bay. He couldn't bear the thought of going home and having Maggie look at him significantly with rolling eyes and raised eyebrows or asking in a stage whisper, "Phil, did you get an answer?"

"I don't want any more letters," he muttered to himself as he scuffed along the sidewalk, "from anyone. I hope no one ever finds the green bottle."

He picked up a pebble and tossed it ahead of him into the water. "But then what?" he asked himself as he walked out on the long dock as close to the edge as possible. He didn't care if he dropped the mail into the bay or fell in himself. The empty day, the day without a kite, stretched ahead of him endlessly, as though he could keep on walking and walking and never walk off the dock into the water. And how many more such days would follow? He might have to do something desperate like . . . He couldn't say the word even to himself, yet.

"Hi, Phil, want to see what I caught?" He hadn't noticed Albert sitting at the edge of the dock, leaning against a piling. "Wait a minute," said Albert. "I think I've got another bite." His fishing line was taut, and his rod was bent down toward the water. He gave a jerk and reeled in quickly. A small, shining fish twisted and flopped at the end of the line.

"Why don't you try?" said Albert, catching hold of the fish. "I've got my handline here."

Fishing! How would that help him get his silver kite? Unless he could sell . . . No. Not at the rate he caught them.

"I'm busy," he said, wishing he were.

"At what?" asked Albert.

The disbelief in Albert's smile forced Phil to answer him. "Working," he said. It surprised Phil to hear himself. But saying it decided him. He'd go home and ask Dad to let him work. It was the only way he could be sure of getting the kite.

Phil walked back to the house quickly, anxious to get started. $14.95. Actually $15.00 minus five cents. How many hours at $1.50 an hour? Phil figured in his head as he walked. Dividing fractions. His math teacher would be proud of him. Ten hours. That's what it came out to.

If he worked one day from nine in the morning until seven in the evening . . . Phil was still calculating when he turned into the driveway and saw Dad scraping the garage doors. Suppose Dad had changed his mind? Suppose he didn't have any work left for Phil to do?

"Hi," he said to his father.

"Any mail?" said Dad, still scraping.

"For Mom," said Phil. He hesitated. He knew so clearly now what he wanted, but it was hard to say it. "Dad," he said. Dad kept on scraping. "Dad," he said again, and his father looked at him. "What was the work you wanted me to do?" Phil hadn't exactly said he wanted to work, but Dad would know that was what he meant.

Dad put his hand on Phil's shoulder in a pleased, affectionate way. It made Phil glad and at the same time embarrassed. It wasn't easy to say you would do what you had earlier said you would never do.

"Come on," Dad said. "I'll show you. Here, I'll get you another scraper first." He brought one from the garage and led the way to the house. "I'd like you to paint the cellar doors, inside and out. And you must agree to work until you've finished the whole job. Just like a professional painter."

"All right," said Phil, feeling that maybe he'd rather be sitting on the dock fishing with Albert after all.

"The secret of a good paint job," Dad was saying, "is good preparation of the surface. Why don't you scrape a bit and let me see how you manage?" He gave Phil the scraper, and Phil started chipping off bits. "That's fine. Keep it flat. Don't let it dig into the wood." And his father went back to his own scraping.

Since the cellar doors were more like a roof over the steps that led down to the real cellar door, Phil was able to sit on one while he scraped the other. This won't take long, he decided when he started. But when he went back over an area he had already scraped, more loose paint came off. And when he wanted to go into the house to see what time it was, suddenly large flakes of paint started coming off in a very satisfying way, and he decided to do another small section first.

Phil didn't notice Maggie standing on the steps near

him until she spoke. "What're you doing, Phil?" she asked.

"Working," Phil said.

"Working? You are?" Maggie didn't say anything more. She just stood watching him for a long time.

"What about Albert's little sister?" Phil finally said.

"Oh, she's here," Maggie answered.

"Do you think you should leave her alone?" Phil asked.

"I want a clacker." Albert's little sister's nose was pressed against the screen door.

"All right. I'll get you a clacker," said Maggie.

"Clacker for cracker," said Phil. "How stupid can you get?"

"A lot more stupid. Like you." Maggie turned around and went back inside. A few minutes later she was out again. "How much longer are you going to work?" she wanted to know.

"Ask Mom what time it is," Phil said. Just then the whistle sounded at the firehouse. It always did on Saturday.

"It's twelve o'clock," said Maggie.

"I know," said Phil. "Hey, Dad," he called out. "When did I start working?"

"About ten o'clock," his father called back.

Ten o'clock. Two hours! That was $1, plus $1, plus two fifties. Three dollars. Only $11.95 to go.

"I think I'll have lunch, Dad."

"Go ahead."

"And then I'll work this afternoon."

"Splendid," his father called.

"You're going to work some more?" Maggie asked.

"I have a lot left to do," said Phil.

"But Albert's little sister has to go home and take a nap," Maggie said. "Can't you play with me?"

"Not till I'm done working," Phil said.

In the afternoon the work seemed much harder. The sun had come around so that it shone directly on the cellar doors. The sweat rolled down Phil's arm as he scraped, and the bits of dried paint stuck to his sweaty legs. When Maggie came to watch him again, he asked her to see what time it was.

"Two-fifteen," she said when she came back.

Two-fifteen! But he'd only started at two o'clock. He felt as though he'd been working for at least an hour.

"Are you sure?" Phil put down his scraper and shook his hand. It was getting stiff from gripping the handle.

"I'll check," said Maggie. The screen door banged behind her. Then she was back.

"It's two-twenty now," she said. "Want to go swimming? Mom's ready to watch us." How Phil longed to dive into the water and wash away the sweat and the scratchy paint and the stiffness. He looked over at his father.

"Dad, can I go swimming?" he called.

"It's up to you," said Dad. Of course it was. He was doing this work voluntarily. And he'd already worked two hours in the morning.

"Come on." Maggie hung over the railing, shaking her pigtail like a tempting little imp. Phil scraped thoughtfully. A big flake flew up in the air.

"No," Phil said. "Later. I'll go at four o'clock." Four hours altogether. That left six hours still to go. Another day. No, probably a day and a half. He could earn all the money for the kite and save his allowance. "I think I can do it, Maggie," he said.

But Maggie had left. Phil wanted to throw down his scraper and catch up with her. He even stood and then sat down again on the hot cellar doors.

"Want to go swimming later?" his father called over.

"Sure," said Phil. And then it was easier to stay and pick up his scraper and work.

{ A Green Pool }

The problem was (Phil let the scraper drop from his hand onto the cellar door) everyone now assumed that what he wanted to do most in the world was work.

"Are you sad, Phil?" Maggie had asked when he came down to breakfast on Sunday morning.

"Why should I be?" said Phil. He was tired and irritated from having stayed in bed too long. The smooth early-morning hissing of the rain on the sand had put him back to sleep.

"Because you can't work, can you?" She had looked at him curiously, as though working had made him into an interesting monster.

"Sorry you couldn't work today," his dad had said to Phil after dinner that night. "You'll have to carry on without me tomorrow."

And this morning Mom hadn't even asked him if he wanted to go shopping. "We won't be long, Phil," she said, looking toward the cellar doors, where she obviously expected to find him when she returned.

After rearranging his Matchbox toys and then putting them back the way Maggie had left them and swinging in the hammock and going over the dune to look at the ocean, Phil had finally gotten the scraper out of the garage.

Now, as he sat on the cellar doors, his hand perspiring around the handle of the scraper, the area that was rough with old paint looked as big as a football field. The chips of paint, when he poked tentatively at them, seemed permanently stuck to the wood. Maybe it was because there was a hot, dry wind from the west that brought with it a horde of blackflies that Phil found himself thinking about the green bottle. He imagined it turning into a cool green pool, a magic pool from which a hand reached out, like the hand with King Arthur's sword, a beautiful green arm and a green hand that opened slowly, offering him $14.95. Yes, today Phil found himself wishing once again for an answer to his note.

He jabbed halfheartedly at a promising paint chip and gouged the wood. The green pool faded. Working alone wasn't any fun. Especially when it was so hot, even in the shade, and the flies were starting to bite. Why struggle?

Why be uncomfortable? And when it came right down to it, how urgent was his need for a silver kite? He could wait for a cooler day or, after all, for . . . What was it he had wished for that moonlit night? A miracle.

He was halfway across the driveway on his way to put the scraper back in the garage when Mom and Maggie returned from shopping.

With the car barely stopped, Maggie jumped out, her visor over one ear. "Phil," she called out. "Phil! There's a letter for you."

Phil felt the same clutch of excitement that had made him almost drop the mail in the post office. But he called back, "So what? I got a letter on Saturday." Mom had gotten out of the car and was watching them. If he didn't shut Maggie up, she'd begin to suspect something. He waited as calmly as he could while Maggie stumbled toward him. He should have known better than to let Maggie in on his secret. It was the same old problem. Maggie interfering, messing up his plans. Of course, he wanted the silver kite, and as soon as possible.

As Maggie came up to Phil, she held the letter behind her back.

"Give it to me," demanded Phil.

"If you promise to let me see it," said Maggie.

Too bad she'd learned to read. Although chances were it was another letter from his aunt. He wouldn't know until he saw the envelope.

"Give it to me," repeated Phil.

"But I helped," insisted Maggie, "with the—"

If he didn't do something quickly . . .

Phil reached around Maggie and took hold of the envelope. It wasn't difficult. She was short and small enough. The danger was that in getting it away from her, he might tear the letter. Or the money. He gripped her arm and started to bend it.

"Ouch, ouch," she cried out.

Phil kept bending. He rather enjoyed feeling masterful and a little mean. The letter slipped to the sand.

"Phil." Mom's voice was disapproving. "Stop that, and carry in the groceries."

"She wouldn't give me my letter," said Phil as he stooped to pick it up. It wasn't fair for him to get blamed. Although he had gone a little bit too far. As he stood up with the letter, he turned it over and saw that it was addressed to Phillip G.—Phillip G.! Wow! This was it. The answer to the note in the green bottle had actually arrived!

"Mom," Phil heard himself calling. "Guess what?" He always told her when anything exciting happened.

But Maggie's astonished "Phil!" brought him to his senses.

"I didn't mean it," he muttered. "I forgot."

Fortunately Mom was lifting bags of groceries out of the trunk and hadn't heard him. Maggie's stern look seemed to be reproaching him. "It was my idea," Phil defended himself. "I can tell anyone anytime I want to."

He slapped at the flies that were landing like pricks of conscience on his legs. He wished he hadn't asked for money. Hiding something you did that was wrong—well, that your parents wouldn't approve of—wasn't any fun. Right this minute when he wanted to, he couldn't tell Mom. And worse still, the secret bound him to Maggie when he was trying to get free.

"Phil, the groceries," Mom called from the front door.

"When?" said Maggie.

"Later," said Phil, carefully folding the letter and putting it in his back pocket. Maybe Albert's little sister would come over, and he could sneak away and read it in private.

Phil carried the bags of groceries into the kitchen, where Mom was making Maggie help put them away. "How much later?" asked Maggie, following Phil back to the car.

Without answering, Phil picked up a bag of groceries and hustled toward the house, stamping off flies as he went. Maggie was right behind him.

"Why doesn't Maggie have to carry any groceries?" Phil asked, dumping his bag on the kitchen table.

"Because they're too heavy," said Mom.

"Because she's a girl," said Phil.

"When she's older." Mom seemed displeased.

Phil went back for another bag with Maggie behind him.

"Maggie," Mom called, "you're supposed to be putting things away."

Maggie stayed behind reluctantly. Phil could tell she didn't want to let him out of her sight. If he brought the bags in quickly enough, she would be stuck helping Mom while he could escape to read the letter.

The last two bags were slipping perilously low in his arms as he staggered with them toward the door. "Help," he called. Mom got there just as one of the bags was starting to tear.

"Lazy man's load," Mom said as she caught the bag before it crashed.

Like a jet fighter, Phil zoomed through the kitchen, dropping the other bag on his way. *Zoom, zoom*, he hummed to himself as he flew through the living room and out the beach door.

"Phil, wait," Maggie called from the distant kitchen.

Zoom. Phil's feet hardly touched the hot sand as he ran over the dune. He wasn't a jet fighter anymore. He was the silver kite soaring out of Maggie's reach.

Which way to go? North? South? Suppose Maggie followed. Where could he hide in the vast emptiness of the beach? To be fast, that was the important thing. Not to stop and think.

"Phil!" Did he hear Maggie calling from the top of the dune? Well, even if she followed, she'd never catch up with him. He could run faster and longer than Maggie could.

Phil sped down close to the water, where the sand was cooler. Because of the heat and the flies, there weren't many people on the beach. Most of them were south, so Phil ran north. Fortunately the tide was low and the sand was hard. He felt he could run and run, all the way to Point Pleasant. All the way to New York.

He didn't hear Maggie anymore. Without stopping to look back, he knew he had left her behind. But still he ran. Thinking of the letter. Thinking of the miracle—the mysterious hand reaching out of the green pool. Thinking of the silver kite.

When he stopped, it wasn't because he was tired. It was because he couldn't last another minute without reading the letter addressed to Phillip G.

The waves barely broke in the shallow pool where Phil stood for protection from the flies. He was taking a chance. If he dropped the letter or the money . . . He took the envelope out of his pocket and felt it. No coins. Maybe it was a five- and a ten-dollar bill from someone who didn't have the change.

Careful, he said to himself, careful, as he ran his thumb between the flap and the envelope. Suppose suddenly, this minute, he would have enough money to buy the silver kite.

"How will you explain to Mom and Dad?" a nagging voice inside him asked. The question made him uncomfortable, uncertain about what he really wanted as he carefully drew out the contents of the envelope. Just a sheet of paper. No money inside. Of course he'd imagined it wrong. It should have been that the hand reaching out of the green pool was empty. Mocking.

But he had gotten an answer. There was no denying that as a way of mailing a letter the note in the green bottle had worked. He could see right away that the writing was easy to read. It was printing, not script, written with a thick black pen, bold and clear, like the work of good students in his class. (Phil's teacher was always writing on his papers, "Your ideas are good, but I have trouble reading them.") It was the writing of someone close to his own age.

Dear Phillip G.,
I don't have $14.95 to spare. If I did, I wouldn't send it to a complete stranger. And I wouldn't send it when I didn't know what it was for. Have you tried working? When I need money, my mom gives me work to do. You may think work is boring. But it's better than doing nothing. I wish I had work to do now. I'm visiting my dad, and I don't know anyone. I spend a lot of time practicing, which isn't exactly work. But it helps. Please write and tell me what you wanted. And do it soon because I won't be here very long.

Hoping to be your friend,
    Meredith M.
    Box 422
    Ocean Harbor, NJ
P.S. Finding the bottle with your note is the best thing that's happened to me since I came here.

Ocean Harbor. The bottle hadn't gone very far. Just the next town. Phil wondered if people farther away would have been more generous.

While Phil stood in the water reading, spray from a wave splashed up on his shorts. Lucky it didn't reach the letter, Phil thought. Not that it mattered. He probably wouldn't keep it. He didn't need it to remind him that the only way left to get the silver kite was work.

Still holding the letter, he started home slowly. Even close to the water it was too hot to lift one foot in front of another. No miracle, he thought. Only a letter from someone else with problems. Meredith. It wasn't a name he was familiar with. A boy? A girl? If it was a boy, he might write back. But he probably wouldn't. Writing would be worse than working, at least in the summer.

Through the haze of heat Phil saw a figure in the distance that he thought, that he was sure, he recognized. Yellow shirt, braid down the back, sitting cross-legged at the edge of the water, slapping flies. Maggie. Except by walking out to the street, there was no way of avoiding her.

"Maggie," Phil called when he got close enough, "how did you know which way?"

"I watched," said Maggie. "Then I went back to Mom. Then I came. But it was such a long walk. I knew you'd have to pass me on the way back."

"Maggie." Phil sat down next to her. He couldn't help feeling pleased. Maggie had followed him. "Want to see the letter?" he said. It was so much more fun to show it to someone. And since there wasn't any money involved . . . "But remember. Don't tell Mom and Dad."

Maggie didn't have any trouble reading it, except she needed help with the name, "Meredith." In fact, she read better than Phil had when he was seven years old. When Phil would complain, "Why's it so easy for Maggie?" Mom would answer, "Because she has you to help her."

Phil didn't know how he would explain about the money, but Maggie didn't seem interested in that part of the letter. "What are you going to say?" she asked.

"What do you mean?"

"What are you going to say when you answer her letter?"

"Her? How do you know it's a she?" demanded Phil.

"Meredith. Meredith." Maggie repeated the name to herself. "I just know," she said. "Meredith," she almost sang. "Meredith is a girl."

That decided it. If there'd been any doubt, there wasn't any now. "I'm not going to," Phil said.

"Not answer it!" Maggie shook her pigtail back and forth in agitation. "But she said she's lonely."

"She didn't say it." Phil stood up, frantically slapping at the flies on his legs. "And it's none of your business."

"But she meant it." Still shaking her head vigorously, Maggie confronted Phil. "And it's mean not to write."

"Oh, forget it," said Phil. He was impatient to get away from the flies, and Maggie.

"But, Phil"—Maggie grabbed his arm—"isn't that where she's from? What she said at the end? Ocean Harbor?

That's not far away, is it? We could invite her over."

"Maggie!" Phil jerked his arm away, aghast at the thought. Someone he'd never met. Someone who might be a girl, maybe a lot older. Someone named Meredith. "Would you please stop messing around in my life!" Phil shouted at Maggie so loudly his voice cracked.

"I don't care about you," Maggie shouted back.

"I don't care. I don't care," Phil heard her calling as he started running. Despite the heat, Maggie's voice and the flies lashed him on. "I want her," was the last thing he heard Maggie calling. "I want Meredith."

After lunch, he resolved, he'd go back to working. And once and for all he'd forget about the green bottle.

Phil paused for breath. But as he looked ahead, a wave sliding slowly up the beach seemed to form itself into a green pool. There was no arm or hand this time. Instead Phil saw a face—drowned, needy, with a mass of hair flowing around it. And Phil thought he recognized the reproachful green eyes of the girl, Meredith.

{ Had Maggie Seen It? }

He tried long sleeves. He tried Mom's old beach hat in which he felt very silly. He tried insect repellent. But the flies still succeeded in finding spots that were unprotected. Moreover, the afternoon sun shining directly on the cellar doors and abetted by the scorching wind from the west had made the doors too hot to sit on. Too hot even to touch.

Mom stood on the front porch, watching Phil hop from foot to foot.

"Ouch," he cried. "Ouch." He wasn't sure which was hurting, the flies or the burning wood. But he wanted Mom to know that it wasn't easy.

"Try it later this afternoon, Phillie," she advised. Her voice sounded sympathetic. "It should be cooler by then."

Phil waited until she left before he quit. It was humiliating. After he'd announced at lunch that he'd be working all afternoon.

He went into the house, closing the screen door quietly behind him. Standing just inside, he heard a broken humming, like a sputtering engine, coming from under the wicker couch. Maggie was exercising the Matchbox toys. He tiptoed into the kitchen. No Mom. She'd probably gone upstairs for a rest. He'd take one himself in the porch hammock until it got cool enough to work.

Phil tiptoed back through the living room. Maggie's legs stuck out from under the couch, kicking lazily as she hummed. Out on the porch it was warm but shaded. It was a relief to lie in the hammock and swing idly back and forth. Phil watched the bumblebees crawl in and out of the trumpet vine on the other side of the screen. He pushed with his foot against the side of the porch to make the hammock swing. It was too bad, he thought sleepily, when he wanted to work not to be able to—

The screen door banged. "Hello!" a voice called. Phil almost fell out of the hammock. "Hello!" again. It was Albert.

"Hi!" Phil called back through a yawn. He must have been asleep. He was perspiring, and his body felt uncomfortably heavy.

Phil heard Albert's footsteps progress through the living room and stop at the porch door. "Want to go fishing?"

said a voice from above the hammock. Nothing kept Albert away from the bay. Even when the rain sent boaters and sunbathers indoors, he could be found seated on the dock cloaked in a yellow slicker. And he never stopped trying to make converts.

"Where's your little sister?" asked Phil. He was so limp he could hardly mouth the words.

"She says she feels clummy—she means crummy—because of the heat. Mom thinks she'd better stay home."

"I do," said a muffled voice.

"What!" Albert clearly hadn't noticed Maggie under the couch in the living room. A sound of scrambling, and Maggie's voice was clearer.

"I'll go," said Maggie.

"You," Phil hooted. That woke him up. "You can't even wait for crabs, and fish take much longer." Phil felt the hammock being jerked from under him. He clutched the sides to keep from tipping out.

"I'd like to try," said a voice close to his ear as Phil put out his foot to keep the hammock from crashing back into the wall.

"You'll roast," said Phil.

"There's a lot of wind," said Albert. "And it's cooler by the water."

"Not with a life jacket," warned Phil.

"I don't care," said Maggie, running off to get it.

Phil gave a satisfied push to the hammock. When he was Maggie's age, he'd already passed his swimming test. Until she did, Maggie had to wear a life jacket on the yacht club docks. Maybe he'd go along, for the fun of being there without one. But he was angry at Maggie. And she might start talking about the note.

"Phil." Maggie was back on the porch.

"What is it?" Phil answered irritably.

"Well . . ." Maggie paused.

"What?" said Phil.

"Well . . ." Maggie paused again. "Are you going to stay in the hammock for a while?"

"Probably," said Phil. "What's it to you? You don't want a turn now, do you? If you're going fishing?"

"No," said Maggie. She seemed preoccupied. She ran out of the porch, calling to Albert, "I'll be right back."

Phil heard the drawer to Mom's desk open and close. Then he heard Maggie go upstairs.

"Sure you won't come?" Albert was standing next to him.

"I might." Phil put one foot on the floor experimentally. Then the next. Then slowly, slowly he stood up. His head felt like an inflated beach ball.

"I couldn't stay long." He was feeling "clummy," like Albert's little sister.

"Okay." Maggie was back. She had her life jacket and visor on and her pocketbook strapped around her waist.

"You won't need that." Phil pointed to the pocketbook.

"I might," said Maggie.

"Phil's going to come," said Albert. Phil felt like an unwary fish that had been hooked.

"What?" said Maggie. "Phil?" She looked surprisingly upset.

I guess she's still angry at what I said on the beach, thought Phil.

"What about working?" said Maggie as though Phil's work were the most important thing in the world.

"Yeah," said Phil as he dropped back into the hammock. It felt so good to lie down again. "When it gets cool, I've got to work."

"That's good, Phil. Good for you," said Maggie. "Come on." She pulled Albert along. "Let Phil rest. He has to work."

"Another time," said Albert as he followed. He never gave up.

With his eyes closed in bewilderment, Phil heard the screen door open and slam shut. Why was Maggie so interested in his working? There was something strange about her behavior. What was it? Why? He'd never figure Maggie out, Phil concluded as he again drifted off to sleep.

When Phil woke, the sun wasn't much lower. Hammocks weren't comfortable enough to sleep in for very long. The blinds on the porch slapped back and forth as the hot wind blew across him. Otherwise silence. Where was everyone? Maggie? Mom? Gradually Phil remembered.

He pushed the hammock back and forth, trying to dispel a feeling of unease. Looking vaguely out at the trumpet vine, he searched for an explanation. The green leaves reformed themselves into the green bottle. And then the green bottle dissolved itself into the green pool, cool and inviting, but troubling. In it he again saw the face, the eyes of an imagined Meredith.

She's not my responsibility, Phil reasoned to himself. He was standing now, shakily. She's not. The more vehemently he insisted, the more uncomfortable he felt.

He had somehow gotten as far as the living room. Since

Maggie and Albert had left him alone, he could at least . . .

He went over to Mom's desk and opened the drawer where she kept the postcards. He picked out one of a sea gull flying. It made him think of the silver kite.

"Dear Meredith." No, he wouldn't write that. Whether Meredith was a boy or a girl, either way, it seemed too familiar. Just:

I wanted $14.95 to buy a silver kite. Now I am working. I'm glad you found the bottle and my note.
      Phillip G.

There. When he read it over, Phil felt that it said all that needed to be said. The pool with the face already seemed to be reshaping itself into an everyday green bottle. A bottle that could be thrown back into the ocean and forgotten.

"I'll mail it right away," Phil decided. "And then I'll go see if Maggie and Albert have caught—" He corrected himself. "And then I'll come back and work."

Phil took the postcard up to his room to address it. Strange. He thought he had left the letter in the envelope. But it was lying open on the bureau. Had Maggie been reading it? Showing it to Mom? No. He'd have heard about that. He could ask her. He would. No. He remembered their argument on the beach. He'd written an answer. The bottle had been thrown back. Best to hope that Maggie would lose interest.

As he crossed the beach to Downer Street and sat down to put on his sneakers, Phil thought: It's a lucky thing I got this done when Maggie wasn't around. Otherwise . . . He knew what it would have been like. Maggie looking over his shoulder, Maggie asking questions, Maggie telling him what to write.

Phil was admiring the picture of the sea gull and reaching for the handle of the post office door when he bumped into Albert. Albert was just coming out, followed by Maggie. They all stood with their jaws hanging down, no one knowing what to say.

"Excuse me." A woman carrying a beach chair pushed past them.

Phil recovered enough to hold the postcard behind his back. Had Maggie seen it? But Maggie and Albert seemed anxious to get away. Perhaps they had left lines in the water. If so, why were they in the post office? What could possibly have drawn Albert away from his fishing rod? They didn't say anything. To Phil's relief, they just left.

"Catch any fish?" Phil felt safe enough to call to their backs.

"No," Maggie called over her shoulder.

"A few bites." Albert turned and stopped to explain. "One was a big one. We almost got him. We could see him. But he dropped the hook. The big ones are clever. But—"

"Come on," Maggie urged, pulling at his shorts.

Phil was glad he had enough money for the stamp.

"Do you want one with a flag? Or one that says 'Love'?" asked the postmistress.

Love! "A flag," muttered Phil.

As he pasted the stamp on the postcard, he looked around to see if by some mischance Maggie and Albert had returned. Except for Phil, the post office was empty.

"All set?" asked the postmistress, reaching for the shutter that covered the window.

It was later than he'd realized. Lucky, thought Phil. Lucky again. But that was close.

He chuckled to himself as he slipped the postcard into the out-of-town slot, remembering the astonishment on Maggie's face.

"That," he said as he left the air-conditioned shade of the post office behind and set out along the burning pavement, "is the end of the green bottle. Now it's time to go back to work."

CHAPTER 9

{ The Second Postcard }

Why was Maggie continually running to the front door? Even Mom asked her whom she was expecting. Phil knew it wasn't Albert's little sister, who was always delivered by way of the beach at the back door.

And there was another mystery. Albert had phoned that morning wanting to talk to Maggie. "Yes," "no," "not yet." That was about all Maggie said. Then she hung up the receiver quietly and went, once again, to look out the front door.

"What did he want?" Phil asked suspiciously. Albert had never called Maggie before.

"His little sister's coming over after her nap," said Maggie, continuing her vigil at the door.

Still, it was strange. Maggie usually made plans with Albert's mom.

All that day, whenever Phil looked up from his scraping, Maggie was standing at the screen door, staring out, or standing on the front porch, alternately watching him scrape and glancing toward the driveway.

"What is it, Maggie?" Phil asked more than once.

"Just looking," she always answered.

Wednesday after breakfast she was at the door again until Mom sent her up to make her bed.

"And have it done when I come back," Mom said. "I won't be long. I'm just going across the bridge for corn. You're in charge, Phil."

As the car pulled out of the driveway, he got the scraper from the garage. Another good day for working. Phil stood above the cellar doors, looking with a now-practiced eye for loose bits of paint. $1.50 on Monday. $3.00 yesterday. That was $10.50 so far. Once he did the outsides, Dad wanted him to do the undersides of the doors. Then at last they would be ready for painting. Finally the job would be finished, and he would have enough money to buy the silver kite.

There! Phil spotted a whole area on the side by the shower that he'd missed. He knelt under the shower and started scraping. Because the concrete hurt his knees, he changed to sitting. Finally he stretched out on his stomach to get to the part where the wood met the foundations. Dad couldn't say he wasn't being thorough.

"Phil," Maggie called, "where are you?"

"Here." He waved an arm. Lying close to the ground, he was hidden by the slope of the doors. He should have let Maggie think he had disappeared. That would have given her something to look for. It was a few minutes before he heard her go inside. Phil knew she had been back at her observation post. For what?

"Maggie," he called after her, "what's happening?" But she didn't hear him. Or she didn't choose to answer.

Maybe it was because he was scraping that Phil wasn't aware that anybody had arrived until he heard knocking at the front door. At first he thought the noise was Maggie coming out again. But then he distinctly heard knock, knock, knock.

It didn't happen often. Maybe once or twice a summer, someone knocked on the front door. Usually the person was collecting or selling something. Mom contributed to the first and got rid of the second. "You're in charge, Phil." What should he do? Pretend that Mom was there but couldn't come to the door? Tell this person to come back another time?

Knock, knock. Nobody was answering. Where was Maggie?

Slowly Phil got to his knees to see who was there. But in an instant he lay down flat again. He'd seen a girl. A stranger. But the worst part was that the hand toward Phil that hung by her side held a green bottle. It didn't take much to figure out who it was. Maggie was right. Meredith was a girl who, at that very moment, was knocking at their front door. He'd done it to himself with the note in the green bottle. He'd conjured up a living human being.

How did she find me? Phil wondered.

Maybe she'd give up and leave. But she was persistent, knocking again and calling out, "Hello! Hello!" It couldn't be long before Maggie would answer. Hadn't she been chained to the front door for two days?

"Hello. Anybody there?"

A living human being. Someone he'd have to talk to. If Mom got back, how could he explain this girl, Meredith, without telling about the note?

Phil turned his head, looking around for a way out. Blocked by the house. Blocked by the cellar doors. Blocked by the bayberry bushes. The only way was the path leading directly to the front porch. Or escape might be possible if he could crawl across the shower without being seen and sneak out onto the beach. He could come back in a couple of hours, by which time she surely would have left. But what might she have told Mom in the meantime?

How had she found his house when the address in the note only had a box number? That was a mystery. And there was the other mystery: Maggie apparently waiting for somebody. But if that person was Meredith, why didn't Maggie answer the door?

For whatever reason, Maggie was doing the right thing now: staying out of sight. Eventually the girl would give up and go away. The knocking had stopped. Perhaps she had left.

Cautiously Phil raised his head above the cellar doors. Then it all happened in a flash. He saw the girl. And the girl saw him.

"Hi," she called. "Didn't you hear me knocking?"

"I was working," said Phil.

"Working," she said, laughing. "Working. Were you really!" She had a bright, caroling voice. "Then you must be Phillip G."

"I am," Phil assented huskily, holding up the scraper as evidence that he really had been working.

"And I'm Meredith," she said as she bounced down the steps and over to the cellar doors. Phil had changed from lying to sitting, concealment now being pointless and escape futile.

"Scraping?" she said, looking down at the doors.

"Yes," said Phil.

"I only get to do that at my grandparents' farm."

"Oh," said Phil.

"I live in New York," she explained, "and go to the farm in the summer. Except I'm visiting my father right now. Mind if I sit down?"

"No," said Phil. There wasn't anything else he could say. Besides, there was something generous, enveloping about Meredith that was hard to resist. She moved in on you like a friendly Labrador retriever bringing back sticks or balls.

In Meredith's case it was the green bottle. "Here it is," she said, handing it to Phil. Then she flopped onto the cellar door and spread her skirt around her.

Phil put the bottle down on the concrete quickly as though it were too hot to touch.

"I wouldn't have found it if Dad hadn't been working late." As she talked, Meredith patted the tight curls on the top of her head. "And I was so bored. Nothing to do but practice. I'd been doing it all day. Finally I gave up waiting for him to drive me. 'Bye, Dad,' I said. 'I'm going for a walk.' And I walked all the way to the beach and straight down to the water. Just at that moment a wave washed the bottle right to my feet as though it was delivering it to me.''

While Meredith was talking, Phil saw the screen door open and a small figure with a visor practically covering her face creep quietly to the edge of the porch and crouch there, listening.

''Wasn't it luck? Imagine if I'd come earlier, or later, or another day.''

Then someone with money might have found the bottle, thought Phil. But he regretted even thinking it when Meredith said, bouncing her hand enthusiastically, ''Then I wouldn't have met Phillip G.''

Phil had to be pleased that the green bottle had helped Meredith, even if it hadn't helped him.

''Phil,'' said Maggie in a small voice as she opened the screen door and stepped out on the front porch.

Meredith turned and stared at her. ''Haven't I seen you before?'' she said. ''Hiding behind a couch?'' There was no answer from Maggie. But Meredith didn't seem to care. Spreading her arms out wide, she leaned back against the slope of the doors.

Why had Maggie been hiding behind the couch? ''Maggie,'' Phil scolded, ''why didn't you answer the door?''

''I'm sorry,'' said Maggie.

''You should be,'' said Phil. ''She might have left.''

''Oh, no,'' said Meredith lazily. ''I was going to stay till I'd returned the bottle to Phillip G.''

''It's something else,'' said Maggie.

''Maggie, speak up. I can barely hear you,'' said Phil.

''Can you come over here?''

"Why?"

"So I can whisper something."

"It's not polite to whisper in front of—"

"Phil!" Maggie's voice was changed, loud with warning.

"What?" said Phil. But he knew where to look. Mom's car was turning into the driveway.

"Quick," he said.

Meredith sat up. "What's happening?"

"I want to show you the beach—"

"But I—"

"Come on." Phil actually took Meredith's hand and pulled her up from the cellar doors. She was unresisting, but a lot heavier than Maggie.

"Phillip G., what is going on?" she said, following him along the boardwalk by the side of the house, up to the top of the dune.

As he looked back, Phil could see Mom's car coming to a stop near the house. Still not far enough. "Let's go down to the water," said Phil. And then, after a minute of looking over his shoulder, he said, "Let's take a walk." No one was following. Not even Maggie. But he'd feel safer farther from the house.

"It's much more fun walking with somebody," said Meredith, happily taking long strides by his side. Phil had to walk quickly to keep up. "I wanted a friend," she said, "at least one. Before I left."

"I want a silver kite," said Phil.

"Do you know what it will look like?" asked Meredith.

"Yes," said Phil. "It has a red dragon on it."

Meredith's skirt swished against him as she walked. It

was black with large red flowers. It made Phil think of the silver kite.

"Sounds exciting," she said. "A dragon in the sky."

Phil stopped and looked back. Still nobody following. Still no Maggie, although he had rather expected her.

"I have a silver flute," announced Meredith.

"A flute," said Phil. "That you play?"

"Yes," said Meredith, sitting down on the dry sand. "And I try to make it sound like silver."

Phil looked around. Nobody he knew in sight. He guessed it was safe to sit down next to her. They were silent. Phil looked at the ocean, while Meredith scooped up handfuls of sand. Finally Phil spoke. "There's silver on the water," he said, "especially early in the morning."

"And in the shells," said Meredith, showing him a blue mussel shell lined with silver.

Phil looked at the ocean and wondered why he liked being with Meredith. She had everything against her. She was bigger than he was. Not heavy, but taller by a head for sure and solid. She'd be a great football player, he decided. She was older. He was certain of that without asking. And she was a girl. Despite all these drawbacks, Phil felt that if he had a silver kite, he'd let Meredith fly it.

He pictured Maggie as he'd last seen her, a pathetic figure wilting under her visor on the front porch. Why hadn't she escaped along with them? Maggie! He stood up. Had she stayed behind to tell Mom about Meredith, about the note? And the bottle. And the money. The note was still on his bureau. The incriminating evidence.

"We've got to go," he said.

"But we just came," protested Meredith, who was by now reclining on the sand, her head resting on her arms. She looked like a rare sea creature washed up by a storm. How would he ever explain her to Mom?

"Isn't it time for you to go?" he asked. He didn't at all want her to leave. But it would remove a problem if she did.

"Don't worry," she said. "Dad doesn't. He knows I can take care of myself. And besides, he's working now. He'll be relieved not to have me hanging around."

"But what about getting home?" asked Phil. "Isn't he coming for you?"

"I'm walking," said Meredith.

"Walking!" exclaimed Phil. "To Ocean Harbor?"

"That's how I got here. I do it all the time in New York when the bus doesn't come." Meredith yawned and closed her eyes. She was clearly not inclined to move.

Should he go without her? Run back to check on what's happening. But Mom would ask questions. And what would he answer?

Phil lay down flat on the sand, his cheek resting on his arm, his head turned away from Meredith. Life would be simpler if she'd disappear. But when he looked back at her, he was glad she hadn't.

After a bit she said, "You should see my flute teacher. He has the reddest face. When he plays, he looks as though he's going to explode."

Then Phil told her about how the kite man's hair stuck out at the sides.

Then they both sat up, and he taught her to play cut the cake.

It was Meredith's turn, and Phil had left it so that the next slice of cake, mixed and molded from damp sand, would surely make the stick candle fall.

"Phil." Maggie was standing behind him. She had changed into her bathing suit, but her face was still covered by the visor. Phil wondered how she managed to see. "Mom wants to know whether you'd like to go swimming," she said.

Phil jumped up and dragged Maggie down toward the waves, leaving Meredith to take her portion of sand cake. "What did you tell her?"

"I said I'd ask."

"Not that. You know what I mean."

"Nothing," Maggie whispered.

"Nothing?" said Phil, sounding like a famous criminal lawyer. "I find that hard to believe."

"Only that . . ." He could barely hear what Maggie was saying.

"Yes?"

"That *she* was a friend of yours. Nothing about the note in the bottle."

"You're sure?"

"I promised, didn't I?" said Maggie, pushing the visor back a bit.

"Good," said Phil. He was pleased with Maggie. At the same time he wondered uncomfortably why she acted as though someone had let the air out of her.

"What shall I tell Mom?" asked Maggie.

"Meredith doesn't have a bathing suit."

"Yes, I do," called Meredith. She was standing up, shaking the sand out of her skirt. How much else had she heard? Phil decided he wasn't very good at conspiracy. "I've got a suit," she said.

"Where?" asked Phil, imagining a green bathing suit stuffed into the green bottle. Meredith pulled the top of a red bathing suit out of one generous pocket and the bottom out of another.

Now what? Mom ready to watch them. Meredith ready to swim. How could he prevent the encounter? He wasn't the famous lawyer anymore. He was the criminal being led away to prison.

Maggie walked way up on the soft sand while Phil and Meredith walked together by the water.

"I won't tell either," said Meredith suddenly.

"About what?" said Phil. Although he knew. And he knew that she knew. He looked at her miserably, wondering what she must think. She smiled back at him in a friendly, nuzzling way.

"But if you didn't want your mom to know about the note in the bottle, why did you send the second postcard?"

"Second postcard?" said Phil. "From me?"

"Yes, asking me to come over. Giving me your address."

Wow! thought Phil. That was it. Maggie expectant by the front door. Maggie and Albert leaving the post office looking as though they had walked off one of the "Most Wanted" posters hanging by the counter. Meredith's letter spread out on his bureau when he thought he had left it in the envelope.

But there was still one mystery. Why did Maggie hide? And if she wanted Meredith to come, why did she continue hiding behind her visor?

"What?" said Phil. Meredith was telling him something.

"I couldn't figure it out," she said. "Because the writing was different. One person liked to do things quickly. That person's writing matched the note in the bottle. The other person was very, very careful."

Albert. But of course, it was Maggie's idea. Who did she think she was, sneaking around behind his back? Didn't she realize he'd find out? Wait till he got her alone.

"I know which one you are," said Meredith, laughing as her skirt was splashed by a wave. "After all, you wanted to get a kite quickly. But who wrote the other?"

"Maggie," said Phil grimly.

"Your little sister? Writing like that?"

"She had help," said Phil. "Look out. That wave's going to catch you."

"It's a little one." Meredith jumped over it as she continued. "And she doesn't seem very pleased to see me."

How to explain to Meredith that he planned to duck Maggie (although that was prohibited) the first time he got a chance? Yet he knew he should be thanking her for writing.

"It's okay," he said. And hoped that conveyed it all. Together they looked up toward Maggie, trudging through the hot, dry sand with her visor pulled down, like a knight ready for battle.

"Is she crazy or what?" asked Meredith.

"Mom says she's a normal little sister," said Phil.

"I wouldn't know," said Meredith. "There's only me."

"You're lucky," said Phil.

But at least Maggie hadn't told. At least that. And Meredith said she wouldn't, so he was safe. Mom and Dad would never know about the note in the bottle.

"Can you make it all right with your mom?" asked Meredith. "Or do you want me to vaporize?"

"No," said Phil. "I mean, yes."

"What do you mean?" Meredith gave him a friendly poke. And he poked her back.

"I mean, yes with Mom, and no, don't go." There was no choice. If he would like Meredith to come back again—after all, she'd want to see the silver kite—she must be introduced to Mom. I'll just say she's a friend, he thought. And that's the truth.

When they came up to Mom, who was sitting on the beach with Albert's mother and his little sister, he introduced "my friend Meredith." But in spite of the fact that Mom didn't ask any questions, Phil felt uncomfortable, as though he still had an itch that hadn't stopped itching.

{ Small like Me }

"Maggie," Phil called. "Maaa-gie." He was sitting on the front steps, husking the corn for dinner, and Maggie was supposed to be helping. Since he and Mom had gotten back from taking Meredith home, she'd been avoiding him. Well, Phil knew why. She didn't want to hear what he had to say. But he'd make her. He'd hold on to her pigtail and make her listen.

Meredith had stayed for lunch and all afternoon, and she

was coming back tomorrow, for the afternoon only. She had to practice in the morning.

"I can't take the summer off," she said. "I'd go backward if I did. That's what Monsieur Dumont says. 'Never you rest still, mademoiselle. Either you advance or you are in the rear. Never you are in the same place.'"

There was no doubt that Mom liked Meredith. Especially after she met her dad when they took her home. Mom had insisted once she found out about Meredith walking. And Phil had gone along in case Mom asked any awkward questions and because he liked being with Meredith.

Phil shook his head as he ripped the husk away from the next ear of corn. Someone who was older, bigger, and a girl for a friend. He couldn't get over it. And then some more luck. He absentmindedly shook a fat worm into the shrubbery and cut off the mushy brown end of the corn as he remembered. He could still see Mom's pleased smile when she found out that Meredith's father was growing up in Ocean Harbor at the same time she was growing up in Squan Beach. They had even bought sodas at the same drugstore when they were children.

But on the way home Mom had asked the awkward question. They were waiting at the red light by the church. "Meredith seems like a very nice girl," she said. "Very interesting." Phil leaned back against the headrest, enjoying Mom's approval. "How did you meet her?" Mom continued.

Phil didn't even pause to think or breathe. "On the beach," he said. And he kept his head back, trying to act casual.

"Oh," said Mom. "Well, she is a walker." And that was the end of that.

When he thought it was safe, Phil sat up straight and looked out of the window. In a way we did, he convinced himself, through the green bottle. But he wished he'd told Mom the whole story because the itch kept itching, the unpleasant awareness of, if not altogether lying, at least not telling the truth.

If I told Mom, Phil reasoned with himself, she'd make me tell Dad. And he imagined how Dad's eyes would look, as though they had storm clouds in them. He'd be angry about the begging. And he might not pay me. And then I couldn't get the silver kite. Getting the silver kite was now even more urgent because Meredith wanted to see it and she was leaving for her grandparents' farm next Wednesday. In one week.

When Phil and Mom walked into the house, Phil almost tripped over his Matchbox toys. Instead of being arranged in rows under the couch, they were piled in the middle of the living room floor. What was wrong with Maggie? Someone with shoes on, like Dad coming back from New York, could have crushed them.

"Maggie," he called. No answer. Where was she? He looked over at the wicker couch. Another change. The dolls that usually spent the summer sitting or sleeping there were gone. Phil ran upstairs. The door to Maggie's room was closed. "Maggie." He knocked on the door.

"Don't make so much noise," Maggie said, adopting a schoolteacherish voice. "We're taking a nap."

Phil guessed that "we" meant Maggie and the dolls.

Strange again. What was going on? Frustrated, he stood at the door. Barging into someone's room without permission was forbidden.

And now Maggie was leaving him to husk the corn alone when Mom had said they were supposed to do it together.

"Mom," Phil called into the kitchen, "Maggie's not helping."

Phil heard Mom calling upstairs. In a minute Maggie came out. She wasn't wearing her visor any longer, but wearing it all afternoon had left a red mark around her forehead. As she stood on the other side of the bag, struggling both to hold an ear of corn and to pull back the husks, Phil exploded with questions.

"Why did you leave my Matchbox toys in a mess?" he asked. And he hoped Mom heard.

"Because I felt like it," said Maggie, sitting down as far from Phil as she could to work on her ear of corn.

The insolence of her answer. Mom! Phil was about to call. But then he decided he didn't want to get Mom involved, because of his next question, delivered in a loud whisper.

"Who do you think you are, sending a postcard to my friend!"

"She wasn't your friend when I sent the card." Maggie looked at him calmly. She seemed to be regaining her irritating self-assurance.

"You did it behind my back," said Phil. "With Albert."

"Well," said Maggie, "what about you? You did plenty behind Mom and Dad's back."

Phil looked guiltily toward the kitchen window. Suppose Mom overheard. He didn't see her head or hear any sound of dishwashing. Then he jabbed his knife into an ear of corn and almost cut himself. What nerve Maggie had. But he could see where she was right.

"That was different." He struggled to justify himself.

"Why?" demanded Maggie.

"Because it was my idea. And it wasn't right for you to use it," he said. "And anyhow, if you wanted her to come, why did you hide when you saw her?"

Maggie bent her head and spoke to her ear of corn.

"What?" said Phil. "I can't hear you."

Maggie wouldn't look at him. She kept holding the ear of corn in front of her like a microphone. "Because I hoped she'd go away."

"That wasn't very nice," said Phil, even though he'd hoped the same thing himself.

"I thought she'd be small like me," she whispered into the ear of corn. "And lonely." Long pause. "I thought she'd play with me," she said, her head sinking down toward her chest as though she wished for the protection of her visor. "But she acts grown-up."

"You have Albert's little sister," he said. "And Albert." With Meredith for his friend, he could afford to be generous.

He reached into the bag for another ear of corn. It was empty. "Look, Maggie," he protested, "I've done all the corn, and you haven't even finished one ear."

"It's your own fault," said Maggie. "You're so mean."

"Well, you can bring everything in," said Phil, taking a handful of corn silk and sticking it down the back of her T-shirt to show who was boss. But it wasn't any fun. Maggie didn't scream or call out to Mom. She sat perfectly still, keeping her back turned to him.

Phil considered taking his Matchbox toys up to his room for safety, but he thought the living room would look empty without them. So he lined them up in their usual garage under the wicker couch, putting his old favorites first: the red London double-decker bus, the bulldozer, and the silver Rolls-Royce. Maggie came past and didn't bother to step on him, as Phil had expected in return for the corn silk. After a moment he heard her tiptoeing back and forth along the upstairs hall. What was she doing now?

Phil and Mom did all the talking during dinner, while Maggie ate silently. He told Mom about Meredith's flute playing, about her grandparents' farm, about her living in New York. He wanted to tell her as much as he could to make up for what he couldn't tell her.

"Let's play War," Phil suggested to Maggie after dinner. She made him uncomfortable. Not saying anything. Open battle was much less disturbing.

"I'm going to bed," said Maggie.

"But it's not dark yet," objected Phil.

"Are you feeling all right?" asked Mom.

"I'm just so tired," said Maggie dramatically. And maybe for the first time in her life she went up to bed voluntarily.

With Maggie gone, there wasn't much to do. Phil read for a while, then followed her. He wanted to get up early and finish scraping in the morning. He wanted to be ready when Dad got back the next day, Friday, to start painting.

After Phil turned off the light, he looked toward the bureau. He had put the green bottle back in its place. No moon to light it up tonight. But as his eyes got accustomed to the dark, he could see its tall black shape eerily reflected in the mirror behind it.

Now he was sure it was a magic bottle. That was the way magic worked. When you asked for something, you were never certain what you would actually get. He'd asked for a silver kite, and he'd gotten Meredith. That was pretty nice magic, he thought, considering the nasty things magic could do.

What an exhausting day it had been. As Phil slid wearily between the sheets, he knew he'd be asleep as soon as he closed his eyes. But what was this? His feet were stopped halfway. His body tensed as he pushed against an impassable barrier of hard, lumpy, scratchy, cold *things*. "Ouch! Help!" he called, leaping out of bed. He switched on the light. "Mom!" he called as he ran back and pulled away the covers.

"Mom!" Phil sprang out into the hall and shouted down the stairs. "There are dolls in my bed!" Then he heard the gentle click of Maggie's door closing.

"What?" said Mom, running upstairs, laughing.

"Dolls," said Phil, beginning to wish he hadn't told anyone.

Mom was still laughing as she lifted four dolls, dressed in nightgowns and pajamas, from under the bedclothes. "I'll take care of these." She straightened the covers, tucked Phil back in, and turned off the light. "Good thing it wasn't crabs," she said as she kissed him on the forehead. "That's what my sister once did to me." She left carrying the dolls.

She ought to be stricter with Maggie. She should have dragged her out of bed and . . . But imagine. Aunt Brenda. Crabs in Mom's bed. That wouldn't be a bad idea, if he had time to catch them, when he wasn't flying his silver kite.

{ Weather }

Phil fell asleep thinking he would launch an attack against Maggie first thing in the morning. But when he woke up, he found he had a more powerful enemy: the weather. As soon as he opened his eyes, he realized that the light in his room was an ominously uniform gray, no sunlight and shadow. Without lifting his head from his pillow, he could smell the salt air from the sea and feel the chill moisture on the tip of his nose.

Fearing the worst, he sat up in bed and looked toward

the ocean. All he saw was the fog, reaching out for him over the sand dune, through the strands of beach grass. It was destroying his entire day, his entire life. That's the way Phil felt as he threw his head back on the pillow.

Then he jumped out of bed and ran downstairs without bothering to get dressed. No one else was up. He opened the front door and looked through the screen. Was it actually raining? He stepped outside. Nothing was falling from the sky, but already he could feel droplets of water collecting in his hair.

Phil went back into the house, closing the door noisily, on purpose. He wanted Mom to come down and tell him that it was going to clear. Then he would know that he could finish scraping and that the cellar doors would be dry enough to paint when Dad got back tomorrow evening. He went to the laundry room and got a beach towel to dry his hair.

"Oh, it'll burn off by noon." Isn't that what they always said about fog? He looked at the sky for signs of brightness. The atmosphere seemed to be getting darker rather than lighter. It was like a scary movie. It could have been exciting and fun if it weren't for . . . Phil hung up the towel and went back to the living room. He'd see what comfort he could get from calling Weather.

As Phil reached for the telephone, it rang. This early? he wondered. He could see the clock in the kitchen. Only seven-thirty.

"Hello," he said. It was even more like a scary movie.

"Hello. Who's this? Phil? Maggie?" A woman's voice.

"It's Phil," he said. What idiot couldn't tell the difference?

"Oh, Phil, hi. It's Albert and Lucinda's mother. Is your mom up yet?"

Lucinda! No wonder everyone called her Albert's little sister.

"I can go see," said Phil.

"Would you mind? It's somewhat urgent."

"Who is it?" Mom was already halfway down the stairs.

"For you." Phil handed over the receiver.

While Mom talked to Albert's mom, he prowled the house, impatiently waiting for a chance to call Weather. Nothing had changed. The view from every window was the same. Fog.

"Her father's had a heart attack," said Mom as she hung up the phone. "Not a bad one, but she's flying out of Newark this afternoon. And . . ." Her hand was still resting uncertainly on the receiver. "She didn't ask, but I think she'd like it if Albert and his little sister could stay with us while she's gone."

Mom looked toward Phil as though she were asking his advice. Well, he had no problem giving it.

"No," he said, "Mom, don't." That's all he would need to make his life more impossible than it usually was with Maggie. Albert and his little sister around the clock.

"Oh, Mom. Do it, do it, do it, Mom." They hadn't noticed Maggie leaning over the banister. She ran the rest of the way downstairs and threw her arms around her mother's waist. She looked like a wild creature with her hair loose on her shoulders.

"Do it, Mom, please. I'll take care of Albert's little sister. I do it most of the time, anyhow. I'll give her a bath and put her to bed. And read her a good-night story. Mom, it would make me so happy."

At this point, even Phil had to acknowledge that anything that would make Maggie happy would be welcome. But Albert, sleeping in his room . . .

"I'm sure it would, dear," said Mom, pulling Maggie's hair back from her face. "But it's Dad. I don't want to ruin his weekend."

"No," said Phil, "don't take any chances." What would Dad do if he thought his weekend would be ruined? Not come? Play tennis all day? Nothing must endanger the painting of the cellar doors. "No," said Phil. "Don't upset Dad."

"I guess I'd better call him," said Mom. She looked at the clock. "He's probably left for work."

She dialed and waited. Phil couldn't stand the suspense. He walked out into the kitchen, through the dining room, and back into the living room. Maggie was lying on the couch with her head under a pillow.

Would the worst happen? Albert's little sister pushing her boat under everyone's feet. And Maggie protecting her rights, demanding that she have a turn in the hammock, that she have first chance to wash off the sand in the outdoor shower, that she have two cookies because she was smaller.

"No answer," said Mom, reluctantly giving up. "Let's have breakfast. I'll try Dad later, at work." And then, with Phil thinking the danger was over, she said, "What's their number?"

"Five-five-five-four-five-oh-eight." Maggie knew it by heart.

Wondering if this could be happening to him, Phil heard Mom saying, "Louise, would it be any help if . . . As long as Phillip . . ." (That was Phil's dad.) And he knew that was it. Zapped before he'd even fortified himself with a dish of Cheerios.

"I told her I had to check with Dad," Mom said when she hung up. But Phil knew that the thing was as good as done. It was obvious that Maggie did, too.

"Oh, Mom," she said, again throwing her arms around Mom's waist. "I love you, love you, love you so much. You are the best mom in the world."

Phil turned his back on the disgusting scene. If it weren't for Meredith and the silver kite, he'd seriously consider running away from home before Albert and his little sister arrived.

"No," he heard Mom saying as he went upstairs to get dressed. "You might disturb her. She'd be better off sleeping in the dressing room."

As he brushed his hair, Phil looked out the window of his room. Nothing had changed. When a day started badly, it only got worse. For confirmation of his sense of doom, he succeeded in dialing Weather before eating breakfast. "Wow!" he called out as he listened. "One hundred percent humidity!" A 60 percent chance of showers. And partial clearing tomorrow. Would that be enough time for the cellar doors to dry out? No promises. But hope.

After breakfast Phil put on his windbreaker and went out to the beach. Two houses north, two houses south, that was as far as he could see. The ocean itself was hidden and secret except for the white breakers that crept in under the fog and the occasional boat's horn piercing the silence.

Lost in the fog like Phil. Lost in the fog of secrecy. Suppose Dad asked the same question: "How did you meet Meredith?" And looked at him straight, trusting his answer the way he always did. If I had the courage, thought Phil, I'd tell him everything. And he imagined that the moment he did, the fog would disappear and the sun would come out and dry the cellar doors in time for him to paint them. But he knew it couldn't happen that way. Not in real life.

To his surprise he found that he had absentmindedly returned to the house. Instead of going in, he followed the boardwalk around to the front. He scented danger. Like Mom asking him to clean up his room or, worse still, make Albert's bed.

Through the porch window he could hear Maggie's voice, high and excited, talking to the dolls or the Matchbox toys. The dolls had been returned to the wicker couch after breakfast, looking a bit rumpled from their nighttime adventure. Phil wished he hadn't said anything. Just taken them out of his bed and hidden them. That would have served Maggie right.

Drops of water hung like berries on the branches of the bayberry bushes near the house. Behind them glowed the orange blossoms of the trumpet vine. No chance of a hummingbird today, or even a butterfly. Phil felt as though he were the only living creature out in the fog.

It was starting to rain gently when he knelt by the cellar doors to scrape. The paint stuck to the scraper, and the scraper slid awkwardly so that he had trouble getting the proper angle. Every other scrape across seemed to gouge the wood and leave ugly crevices behind.

The water was starting to run down his forehead into his

eyes. It was a miserable place to be, but Phil was afraid he'd be more miserable inside. Maybe he should go and sit in the garage. Maybe . . .

He heard the telephone ring. One ring and Maggie had answered it. As though she'd been expecting a call. No doubt she and Albert were plotting something else together.

"Mom," he heard Maggie shout, "where's Phil?"

"I'm here," said Phil, running up the steps and barely pausing to brush the sand off his feet.

Maggie was holding the receiver just above the cradle as though she were about to hang up.

"Careful, Maggie." Phil snatched the receiver out of her hand.

"It's her," Maggie hissed in a stage whisper.

"Phil?" said Meredith. It was the first time she hadn't called him Phillip G. He liked Phil a lot better.

"Hi," said Phil.

"What're you doing?"

"Scraping," said Phil.

"In the rain? You've got to be crazy." He could imagine her smile as she said it. Perhaps she was bouncing her hand on her hair.

"It's not going well," he admitted. "But if you knew what's happening inside, you'd understand—"

"That's why I called," she interrupted. "I wasn't sure about coming."

Of course, thought Phil. The next terrible thing in this terrible day. No Meredith.

"Dad thought I should ask because it's so wet. For walking, I mean. And he's so busy . . ." Phil was too disappointed to listen until she said, "He can drive me over if your mom would bring me—"

"I'll ask her," said Phil. "I'm sure it's okay."

But Mom, who was usually so obliging about transporting friends, looked worried. "What do I do with Albert's little sister?" she said as she peeled the shell off a hard-boiled egg. "And I haven't reached your dad yet. What's he going to say? But it's too late. They'll be here at lunchtime."

"Mom," said Phil, "Meredith's waiting. If you can't, she can't come," he explained hopelessly.

"It's that"—she held the egg under running water—"everything's happening at once."

If he'd been Maggie, he would have persuaded her by now. Instead he started wordlessly back to the telephone.

"Wait," Mom called after him. "I can go right away. Ask if her dad can pick her up."

"Oh, Mom." If he'd been Maggie, he would have run back and hugged her. Phil hoped she could tell from his voice how grateful he was.

Lunch with Albert's little sister was, as usual, a mess, but Meredith didn't seem to mind. Even when, her mouth smeared with peanut butter and jelly, milk dripping from her chin, Albert's little sister insisted on climbing into Meredith's lap. "Melodith, Melodith," she said fondly.

"Melodith, isn't that silly?" Maggie pulled her visor up to laugh a fake laugh and then pulled it back down.

"I like it," said Meredith. "It's exactly right for me. For someone who makes music."

After that Maggie didn't say anything more. She morosely concentrated on eating deviled eggs and a peanut butter and jelly sandwich without lifting her visor.

Albert managed to eat a lot and ask a lot of questions. "How long do you practice?" he asked Meredith.

"About an hour," she said. "Sometimes two."

"I fish for longer than that," said Albert.

"But you don't have to concentrate." Meredith knew how to handle Albert.

"Melodith, Melodith," said Albert's little sister, putting her sandwich on Meredith's plate.

"I do have to concentrate or the fish won't bite," argued Albert. And he kept asking questions. How long was Meredith's flute? How many years had she been playing? And then he said, "When did you get the postcard?"

My gosh! Albert! The postcard! Phil had forgotten to worry about Albert. How much more did he know? If Mom asked, how could he explain without telling the whole story?

"Let's play Monopoly," he suggested before anyone could think of another question.

"I don't know how," said Meredith.

"You never played Monopoly?" said Albert in his superior way.

"You never played Monopoly!" Maggie came out from behind her visor to express sincere astonishment.

"She plays the flute." Phil defended her, pleased at the success of his diversion.

Meredith didn't need to be defended. "I know. I'm a freak. It's about time I learned."

And Albert's little sister completed the diversion by spilling her milk.

"Thank goodness she takes a nap," said Mom. "Go with

Maggie," she said, shoving her toward Maggie, who jumped up from the table and stumbled into a chair. "For heaven's sake, will you take that thing off so you can see where you're going!" exclaimed Mom.

"I want Melodith," said Albert's little sister.

Maggie stumbled into another chair.

"Melodith is going to play a game," said Meredith, "while Maggie takes you up for your nap." With an air of having settled things, she told Mom, "I've had lots of experience handling my cousins at the farm. You've got to tell them when to get lost."

Maggie didn't come back down. It was okay with Phil, but Mom seemed concerned. "Phil," she called out as she was wiping the dining room table, "go see what's happened to Maggie. She loves to play Monopoly."

"Oh, Mom. I have to explain houses and hotels to Meredith."

They had the Monopoly board spread out on the rug.

Then Phil heard Mom upstairs talking to Maggie, and Maggie shouting, "No, I won't. I want to take a nap," and Mom sounding soothing.

It had been years since Maggie had taken an afternoon nap. She was getting stranger every day. But with Meredith and Albert there, he could play Monopoly without having to wait for her.

When she finally appeared, crawling across the floor by way of the kitchen and dining room, Albert, who had built his first house on Marvin Gardens, announced that it was too late for her to join the game.

"Good. Because I'm not interested," said Maggie, and she left to swing in the hammock.

Phil looked in her direction from time to time, wondering why she didn't come back and pester them. But he forgot her in his drive to acquire all the railroads and both utilities.

"Boop, boop." Albert's little sister was back already. "Boop." Her boat was headed toward Meredith across the Monopoly board.

"Maggie!" Phil called. "Do something with her. Maggie!"

No answer. Phil went storming out to the porch. "Maggie," he said, "didn't you hear—" The visor was lying on the floor under the hammock. Maggie's arm hung loosely over the side. When Phil looked into the hammock, he saw that she had slipped down to the center and was fast asleep.

He could hear Albert and Meredith making plans to go fishing. Suppose they decided to go when he had to work?

"Your turn, Phil," Albert called.

Fishing could be fun with Meredith. Phil sat down thoughtfully in front of his utilities and railroads. He wasn't going to get left out. Even for the silver kite.

"How about Saturday morning?" Albert was saying. "Do you practice then?"

"No," said Meredith. "In the summer I take the weekend off. But won't you be working, Phil?"

"I dunno," said Phil.

"Will you be working all day?"

"No," said Phil. No matter what, he wouldn't work all day.

"Fishing in the afternoon," said Meredith while Phil threw the dice and moved his counter around the board. "And on Sunday maybe Dad'll take us out in the boat. And on Monday the silver kite. Right, Phil?" Her eyes were sparkling.

You get free of one person and you're hooked on to another, he thought. Now he couldn't disappoint Meredith.

"If it stops raining," said Phil. He tossed the rent for Park Place in front of Albert. Then he got up abruptly and went over to the phone.

"Hey," said Albert, "that's not enough. "I have two houses now."

"In a minute," said Phil. For the tenth time that day he dialed the number for Weather.

{ The End of the Tunnel }

Phil waited until they were both in bed. What he had to say was more easily said in the dark. In fact, the night was so dark he couldn't see Albert, just the whiteness of his pillow. He hadn't moved since Phil turned out the light. Phil wondered if he was asleep already.

"Albert," Phil whispered.

"Yeah," said Albert in a normal voice.

"You asleep?" It was obvious that he wasn't.

"No," said Albert patiently.

"Albert . . ." It was hard to know how to start.

"Yeah," said Albert through a yawn.

"Don't say anything more about the postcard."

"Why not?" asked Albert. "Meredith knows who sent it. Maggie told me."

"Yes, we figured it out, but . . . When Dad comes, don't say anything about it."

"Why not?" Albert sounded disinterestedly curious.

"Well," said Phil, "it's complicated." This business of swearing people to silence was making him feel more and more ashamed. "I mean, there's more to it."

"Look, Phil." Phil could hear the springs of the bed creak as Albert turned toward him. "Why don't you tell him whatever it is yourself? Then you won't have to worry about anyone else."

"But it might upset him," said Phil.

"The point is," said Albert with his usual precision, "not how he feels but how you feel." The bed creaked again as Albert turned away. Then, as Phil remained silent, wondering how to respond, he heard Albert's breathing become slower and deeper. That was it. Albert had said all he had to say, and he wouldn't appreciate being awakened.

As his eyes roamed the room, Phil thought he could see the shape of the green bottle, a dark, shadowy sentinel on his bureau. You, he addressed it mentally, you with your miracle got me into this. Now get me out.

No answer. Or was the answer: It's up to you, Phil? Or was Phil's own voice telling him there in the solemn darkness what he had to do?

When Phil woke the next morning, the world looked like a tunnel to him, a wet, dark tunnel that he had resolved to walk through, that he knew he must walk through before he got to daylight. Indeed, it was raining still. If it rained all day, there'd be no possibility of scraping. And if it rained tomorrow, Saturday, Dad's workday . . . No painting maybe all weekend. No silver kite before Meredith left. But then maybe after he told Dad what he planned to tell him, no silver kite ever.

He was as impatient as Maggie had been, looking out the front door before breakfast, between juice and Cheerios, after breakfast.

"Rain before seven, clear before eleven," Mom called from the kitchen.

"I don't really care," said Phil. And in a way he didn't. His fate had been decided. He just had to keep on going through the tunnel. He tried to read a book, but his head kept turning toward the window. After a while he called out, "Blue sky, Mom. Do you see it?"

The wind seemed stronger from the west. "It's a clearing wind," said Mom. The patch of blue sky disappeared, then reappeared, larger.

By 10:56 (Phil looked at the clock before he went out) he was searching out the last bits of loose paint on the cellar doors. He tried to keep the tunnel mood, the mood of dogged resolve to tell Dad everything. But with the sun and the wind triumphant over the laggard clouds it was hard to keep feeling like a guilty penitent. Maybe confession wasn't necessary after all. Maybe it wasn't sensible. What would Meredith do? If he could get her alone this afternoon, he'd ask her.

Seven hours of scraping. $10.50. If the painting took, let's see . . . Phil amused himself by calculating while he scraped. Three hours' more work would bring him exactly what he needed plus five cents. He hoped that was all it took to paint the cellar doors. He didn't want to work a minute longer than was needed to pay for the silver kite.

Phil was surprised when Maggie came out and sat with her legs dangling over the edge of the front porch. She pulled on her pigtail, watching him silently.

"Where's Albert's little sister?" he finally asked.

"Mom's reading her a story." More silence.

Phil tried to think of something to say. It was nice having Maggie there. He wanted her to stay. But he didn't want to talk about Meredith, and he didn't want to talk about the silver kite.

"What's she reading?" he finally asked.

"*Mrs. Tiggy-Winkle.*"

A book for little girls. Although Phil rather liked the pictures of Mrs. Tiggy- Winkle's hedgehog spines sticking out through her cap.

Silence again.

Then: "Is *she* coming?" Maggie gave her pigtail an extra yank as she spoke.

The scraper slipped. Another gouge in the wood. Not a big one. Phil hoped Dad wouldn't notice. Right now it was the least of Phil's worries.

"Who?" he said as he started to give the cellar doors a last, grand going-over. Of course, he knew the answer, but he wanted to make Maggie say it.

"You know." Maggie stubbornly resisted, swinging her feet.

"Yes." Phil gave up. "After lunch for a swim."

"Will she get a turn on the raft?" asked Maggie.

"Of course." Phil rapped the handle of the scraper against the wood for emphasis. "Except maybe we'll double up." It was what he'd always wanted to do with Maggie.

Maggie didn't say anything more. She swung and pulled and looked dreamy while Phil scraped.

"Want clacker. Want Melodith." Albert's little sister was salivating at the door. Maggie scowled and left.

"How about rafting?" Phil asked Meredith when she arrived. He'd waited inside for her while everyone else went out to the beach. First Mom, carrying Albert's little sister. Then Maggie with the raft on her head.

Everyone except Albert, of course, who had already caught two snappers, which he fried for his lunch. "I'll bring enough for dinner," he promised grandly as he left with the rod on his shoulder.

Phil was glad to see him go. It would make it easier to get Meredith alone.

"Sure," said Meredith. She was taking off her skirt, right in front of him, because she'd worn her bathing suit underneath.

"We can do it together," Phil said, "or separately."

"Oh, together," said Meredith, shaking her skirt to the floor.

When they reached the beach, Phil wasn't surprised at what he saw. Maggie was floating on the raft. The water was deep and calm—more swells than breakers. And Maggie was just lazing around, drifting with the swells. It couldn't be very exciting. Phil was sure she'd be tired of it soon.

They spread their towels on the sand away from Mom and Albert's little sister. But it wasn't long before they heard a loud "boop, boop" and a boat was being pushed under Meredith's knees. It didn't matter, though. She wouldn't understand what they were saying.

"Do you tell your parents everything?" Phil asked as soon as they both sat down.

"Melodith, Melodith." Albert's little sister was climbing into Meredith's lap.

"You're too heavy," said Meredith, setting her back down on the sand. "Make it go around. See." She drew a big circle around them and started the boat off herself. "Boop, boop," she said.

"Boop, boop." Albert's little sister grabbed the boat and took up the cry.

"Now, what was it?" She settled back next to Phil.

It seemed harder to ask it again, but Phil did. "I just wondered what you did, whether you told your parents everything."

"Are you kidding?" said Meredith. "With Dad, there's not so much chance to, but still, if he knew . . . Or Mom knew . . ."

"Knew what?" asked Phil.

"Why should I tell you?" teased Meredith.

"I just wondered," said Phil, trying to seem less interested than he was.

"Well, for one thing, what I see on the streets. I'll tell you before you ask me. Like men peeing in the gutter. And worse."

And worse. It didn't take much imagination to guess what that was. Phil didn't say anything.

"I used to be shocked," said Meredith. "I wanted to run and tell Mom right away. But I figured it would upset her. I mean, that's it. If you told your parents everything, they'd get so upset they wouldn't let you move."

"Yes," said Phil. "I guess that's what I think. But I meant more when you'd *done* things they wouldn't approve of."

"Same idea," said Meredith. "You couldn't live in New York without doing things your parents wouldn't approve of. Not things they told you not to do, but things they hadn't thought of."

"Yes," said Phil. "That's it. That's what I wondered about."

"It would only worry them," said Meredith. "And they'd think they had to punish you. Like docking your allowance, which wouldn't be fair."

Or not paying for work. After all, Dad hadn't ever told him not to put a note in a bottle asking . . . Phil felt rather foolish thinking that way.

"Are you about to tell all?" asked Meredith as she set Albert's little sister back on her route.

"Maybe," said Phil. Maggie was coming out of the water. It was a good time to get the raft. And he knew what he wanted to know. He had a choice now. He didn't have to walk down to the end of the tunnel.

They all met where Mom was sitting: Phil and Meredith, with Albert's little sister and the boat at her heels, and Maggie with the raft.

"Our turn," said Phil, taking hold of the rope around the side.

But Maggie hadn't let go. "It's her turn," she said, pointing to Albert's little sister.

"What could she do with it?" Phil was incredulous. "You've had it. And now it's my turn. The way it's always been."

"But she's our guest," said Maggie, lifting a protesting ally onto the raft.

"So's Meredith," said Phil, pulling the raft away so that Albert's little sister ended up with her face in the sand. She started whimpering, but Mom grabbed her before she could get going full blast.

"Meanie," said Maggie. "You're so mean." She picked up the raft and started to loosen the valve.

"Maggie," said Mom sternly, "stop that. And give the raft to Phil and Meredith."

"Meanie, meanie, meanie," said Maggie, jumping up and down on the raft. As she did so, the air came out in puffs. And the raft subsided until it was almost flat.

"Maggie!" said Mom. "Sit down and blow up that raft and stop this nonsense."

"I'll do it," said Meredith. "I'm good at blowing."

Mom took Maggie's hand and pulled her off the raft while Meredith picked it up.

With her other hand Mom pulled Phil to her. "Now look, you two," she said, "I want a change. Maggie, I want you to be nicer to Phil and Meredith. And, Phil, I think it would help if you made more effort to include Maggie."

Include Maggie! That's what he'd been trying to do for years. Not so much now that Meredith was around, but still . . .

"Well?" said Mom.

"I'll try," said Phil, looking at the sand.

"Maggie?" Mom looked at her. So did Phil. She said something Phil could barely hear. But Mom seemed satisfied.

"I've got ten arpeggios' worth of air in here," said Meredith, holding up a plump raft.

"Want to go out with us?" Phil asked Maggie. The water was calm enough. They'd put her in the middle. Then she'd really be included.

"No." Maggie wrote it with her toe in the sand. "Not with her," she mumbled. This time Phil could hear it. But Meredith and Mom didn't seem to.

When they were at last floating tranquilly in the water, Meredith said, "Why do you let these little kids run your life? Just ignore them and do your own thing."

"That's what the silver kite is going to be," said Phil. "My own thing." He looked up into the sky over the beach as he said it. Gone. Nor was there the faintest whisper of a *whiffle, whiffle*. It was up to him now. Next time the sound would come from his own kite.

When they came in from the beach, the phone was ringing.

"Get it, Phil," said Mom, who was loaded down with Albert's little sister. "It might be Dad."

Phil ran up the steps and lifted the receiver in the midst of a ring. Maybe the last one before the caller gave up.

"I'm catching the late train," said his father.

"But—" said Phil.

"Any problem?" Dad sounded impatient.

"Nothing," said Phil. "I'll tell Mom." As he hung up, he said out loud to himself, "It'll be dark when Dad gets home." That meant he wouldn't be able to inspect the cellar doors until the next morning. That might delay everything.

It was all because of Albert and Albert's little sister. Dad didn't want to come until the children had eaten and the younger ones were in bed. "Isn't that right, Mom?" he asked accusingly as she jammed boiled hot dogs into rolls. She didn't answer.

When Mom left to meet Dad, there was still enough fading light over the bay to set off the black silhouettes of the houses. The light at the end of the tunnel. Was he there already? Meredith's way or Albert's way? Maybe they both worked.

In seconds the light disappeared from the sky completely. Darkness after all. He was still in the tunnel. Phil switched on the lanterns by the front door and turned back, blinking, into the living room. He could see Albert seated at the dining room table. Like a judge casting lots, he was laying out the cards for solitaire.

Phil stood behind him and looked at the cards. An ace. "You can put that out," said Phil.

"I know." Albert dealt to the end of the row and then moved the ace.

"You'll have to go to bed when Dad gets back. He and Mom want to have dinner alone."

"I always go to bed at nine-thirty."

"Albert."

"Yes?"

"I talked to Meredith today, and she said—"

Phil heard the car in the driveway.

"Yes?" said Albert again.

"Never mind." Phil heard Dad's city shoes coming up the steps.

"Hello, hello."

"Hi, Dad." Phil lingered behind Albert.

"Let's go," said Dad, putting his briefcase on the chair. "Inspection time."

"Now? In the dark?" It was more than Phil had hoped for.

"Now. Before dinner," said Dad. "I want to look at the work Phil's been doing all week," he said to Mom, who had come in behind him.

There were the kitchen lights shining out through the windows above the cellar doors, the lights on the front porch, and the flashlight from the car. Together they made it bright enough for Dad to see where the old paint had been scraped off the doors. After shining the flashlight in an arc, he switched it off and stooped down to have a closer look. He ran his hands over the surface of the wood, searching out loose bits of paint. "Feels good," he said. "Very thorough."

Phil squatted next to him. The mood of intimacy and approval was too pleasant to interrupt. Nothing need be said now or ever about the green bottle. "I did dig into it in a few places," he felt righteous in adding. "Here." He laid his hand on one of the worst gouges. "It's very rough."

"A bit," agreed Dad, touching it with the tips of his fingers. "But the paint'll fill it in. It's bound to happen." Dad stood as he spoke. He seemed to go up a great distance into the darkness. Phil stood quickly so as to stay close to him.

Dad shone the flashlight playfully in Phil's face. "Any other problems I can solve?" he joked.

Phil pushed the flashlight aside, and to his surprise he

heard himself saying, "Dad, I've done a terrible thing."

There was an instant's pause, and then Dad said calmly, from his great height, "Why don't you tell me about it?" And seeming to sense how hard it was for Phil's tight, nervous voice to reach him, he said, "Let's sit down and talk."

He sat on one cellar door, and Phil sat on the other. Phil could feel the warmth of the day's sun stored in the wood. Dad was looking toward him, but his face was shadowed. How to continue? "I've been begging," said Phil. He decided to start with the worst part first.

"Begging? How?" asked Dad. Phil thought he already sounded relieved.

"With the green bottle."

"The green bottle. Whatever do you mean?" Dad was starting to sound impatient the way he did when he couldn't understand something.

Phil explained about the note and the bottle and the silver kite. "And you helped," said Phil.

"When?" said Dad. Phil hoped he was starting to sound amused.

The more Phil talked, and the more Dad listened, the easier it got. He told about the letter and Maggie and the two postcards. And the appearance of Meredith. And then, since Dad still seemed interested, he told about Albert's advice and Meredith's advice and how he hadn't known what he was going to do until he did it.

"Which was the right thing," said Dad. "Albert's got it right. Although I understand Meredith's problem. Still, I suspect her parents can take more truth than she imagines."

"You mean you're not upset about the note?"

Dad laughed. "You could call it begging. Or you could call it pretty damn clever."

Phil's voice brightened. "And it worked, in a way. Only thing was"—he felt it was safe to be completely honest—"I had to lie to Mom about Meredith."

"You never have to lie, Phil," said Dad firmly. "Go tell her the whole story while I wash." He stood up again, pulling Phil with him. "I'm proud of you, young man. You've done a lot of growing up this summer."

But . . . Phil didn't say anything out loud. He stood there wondering. Wasn't he going to be punished? Wasn't the terrible thing he imagined going to happen? Would he still be able to get the silver kite?

There was a breathless moment when Dad didn't do anything. He didn't say anything. He didn't leave. He simply looked down at Phil with a smile furrowing his face deeply in the shadowy light. Then he said, "Now for some dinner."

Phil followed him into the house. Albert, the judge, was still playing solitaire. Phil sat down across from him. "You were right," Phil said. He was so happy and relieved he could acknowledge it.

"Of course," agreed Albert without even asking him what he was talking about.

{ Chocolate Fudge Icing }

"**N**othing can stop me now," chanted Phil to himself as he slathered paint on the cellar doors. They had been gray, and he was making them brown.

"To match the shingles," said Dad.

He'd finished the hardest part already—the back and sides against the house. And the bottom, where the foundations of the house met the sand. Those had to be done with great care, so as not to get blotches of paint on the shingles or end up with a paintbrush full of sand.

"A little either way won't hurt," Dad reassured him. Phil hoped that the sand he seemed to be spreading around with the paint could be called a little. The nice thing about painting brown over gray was that you could tell where you'd painted and where you hadn't.

Now Phil was painting the undersides of the doors. He painted in sweeps and dabs and made up a song to the tune of "Row Your Boat" to sing while he painted.

> *"Paint, paint, paint the wood*
> *On the cellar door.*
> *Merrily, merrily, merrily, merrily,*
> *Get the kite for sure."*

"Looks good." His father came over from scraping the garage to watch him. "Be sure to keep the paint thin," he advised.

"Then the gray will show," said Phil.

"That's a problem when you change colors. You may need to give it a second coat."

"Me!" Phil almost dropped his brush. "What does that mean?"

"You wait for the first coat to dry, probably about twenty-four hours, and then you put on a second coat," said Dad in his it's-perfectly-simple tone of voice.

"You mean I won't finish today?" exclaimed Phil.

"We'll see," said Dad. "We'll see how it looks when it dries. But remember, you signed on for the whole job." There was no arguing that point, or any other, after last night.

"Keep it thin," his father repeated, "or it will peel off before the summer's over."

Phil painted more slowly and tried to be conscientious about using less paint. But another coat! That would be tomorrow and probably in the afternoon. His father didn't like working on Sunday morning, and he probably wouldn't let Phil work either.

Well, Phil and Meredith had plans for tomorrow afternoon. Her dad had promised them a ride in his boat. Phil could picture it: Meredith, Albert and his little sister, Maggie, Mom, and Dad, everybody. He could picture them going off in the car while he was left painting the cellar doors.

When he had painted the sides and the undersides, Phil stopped for lunch. His hand was stiff from holding the brush for so long. And he was hungry!

"Why, Phillie, painting gives you an appetite," observed his mother when he made up his second tuna fish sandwich.

"I'll be over soon," he told Meredith as she and Albert set off after lunch to go fishing. Phil looked jealously at Albert's back, actually his profile. He was turned toward Meredith, talking. Phil could hear the fading drone of his voice as he explained the strategies of fishing. "And when the float gets pulled under . . ." Phil could imagine him saying.

Phil took his brush out of the turpentine and cleaned it on a piece of newspaper. "I'll make quick work of this," he promised himself. "And then maybe Dad will pay me. And on Monday I'll get the silver kite."

He settled down to paint with the brush in one hand and the paint can in the other. He'd barely started, a bold brown splash against the gray, when Maggie came out of the house, without her visor, and down the steps to where he was working.

"Want some help?"

Maggie? Seven years old? Painting? Phil could barely suppress a guffaw. But maybe this was Maggie's way, after Mom's lecture, of being nice to him.

"Thanks," said Phil. "I've got to do it to earn the money."

"Is it hard?" she asked. She was leaning over the strip he had just painted.

"Look out," warned Phil. She almost had her nose in the paint. "You'll mess it up."

"Smells awful." Maggie unbent herself. "Want me to read a story?"

"To me?" said Phil. As though he were Albert's little sister! But Mom had said to include . . . And painting was more fun with Maggie around. The old, curious Maggie.

"*Mrs. Tiggy-Winkle*," said Maggie. "It's right inside."

Phil almost groaned. But Mom had said . . .

Maggie came back with the book and a little footstool, which she put down next to where Phil was painting.

"Careful," Phil reminded her. "Not too close."

"Mrs. Tiggy-Winkle's nose went sniffle, sniffle, snuffle, and her eyes went twinkle, twinkle." It made Phil think of the whiffle, whiffle of his silver kite.

Mainly Maggie told the story as she remembered it by looking at the pictures. She read *The Cat in the Hat* next, and after that she got her book of riddles and made Phil guess.

"What's big and red and eats rocks?"

"A big red rock-eater."

They were so dumb. If he didn't already know the an-
swers, he'd never guess them.

"All right," he said at last. "That's it." He stood back to
admire his work. "Doesn't it look great, Maggie?" he said.

"What are you going to do next?" She closed the book
but still sat on the stool.

"Go fishing," said Phil briskly.

"I thought you didn't like to fish." Maggie was getting
that hangdog look again.

"Why don't you come, too?" suggested Phil.

"I can't," said Maggie. "It's almost time for . . ." She
looked toward the house.

Phil knew she meant Albert's little sister, who was already calling from her cot bed for "olange juice." Poor Maggie. But . . . "You wanted her to stay here," he said.

"Yes, I did," said Maggie, "and I don't want to go fishing." She picked up her stool and marched into the house.

"Is that enough?" Phil asked anxiously when Dad came
over to examine the cellar doors. Undeniably there were
places where the gray showed through the brown. But not
many, in Phil's opinion.

"It's a good paint job," said Dad. "The best that can be
done in one coat."

"Then it's finished? I'll have enough money for the kite
now."

"We'll see," said Dad. "We'll see how it looks when it
dries."

That was exactly what he'd said before.

Even if it wasn't perfect, Phil was proud of his paint job.
In fact, he had trouble tearing himself away from it to go
fishing.

"It looks like chocolate fudge icing," he told Albert and Meredith when he found them at the end of the long dock.

Meredith sat cross-legged with her skirt tucked around her. "This is real work," she said.

"Not as real as painting," said Phil.

"Well, harder work than practicing the flute. Waiting is work for me."

"I told you," said Albert. "And you've got to watch all the time."

"But it's forever," said Meredith. "Time goes faster if you're doing something."

"It's like that with painting," said Phil. He couldn't stop remembering the smooth sheen of the cellar doors.

"Just wait till you see them," he said as they walked back together.

Albert carried a bucket with his two fish. No one else had caught any. "Next time," he had promised Meredith. "It takes experience." Now he said, "I'll clean them at the shower."

"No," Phil snapped. "No one can use the shower. Dad said so. Because of the fresh paint."

He pointed toward the cellar doors as they turned into the driveway. Maggie was standing in front of them, and next to her was Albert's little sister.

Maggie was pointing. Phil could hear Maggie's voice instructing her the way she did the dolls and the Matchbox toys. Suddenly she was reaching, and Albert's little sister was teetering. Or was it the other way around?

And then there was the most awful wailing Phil had ever heard in his life. Everybody ran. Mom from the house, Dad from the garage, Phil, Meredith, and Albert up the driveway.

The crying came from Albert's little sister. Phil expected that. He also expected blood, a major injury. What else could account for such howls? But instead . . . He was not prepared for what he saw. Albert's little sister was sitting on the cellar doors, her plump legs out in front of her, the palms of her hands resting on the wet paint.

"Wa-a-a-a, wa-a-a-a!"

"I didn't push her," said Maggie, who was trying to pull her up.

"Wait," said Mom. "Let's wipe her hands before she gets the paint on her face."

"I didn't push her, Mom," said Maggie.

"Rags. That's what we need," said Dad, running back to the garage.

Albert quietly slipped in the front door with his fish, as though he'd seen it all before and wanted to escape as quickly as possible.

"I didn't push her," Maggie kept repeating. And the more she said it, the more Phil believed he had seen her do it.

When Dad came back with the rags, Albert's little sister was lifted off the cellar doors and given a preliminary wiping. Meredith took one leg; Mom took the other. Maggie looked on without saying anything more.

"A little turpentine," said Dad. "She'll be as good as new."

"Except for her bathing suit," said Mom. "It may be ruined."

"What about my doors?" The words exploded out of Phil.

Everybody stopped looking at Albert's little sister and turned to the cellar doors.

"Look." Phil pointed. "Look at that."

A big blotch of gray where she had sat down. Two gray hand prints. Two smears for legs.

"Oh, Phil, what a shame," said Meredith.

"That's too bad, dear," said Mom.

"It's tough," said Dad. "But they would have needed a second coat anyhow."

"I didn't push her," said Maggie once again, her head hanging down.

"Yes, you did," said Phil. "You did. I saw you." He knew clearly now how it had been. First Maggie's arms shooting out. Then Albert's little sister falling. "I know you did."

Phil tried to get past his mother to Maggie. He wanted to shake and shake and shake her.

"Phil." Mom put out her hand. "I'm sure Maggie is telling the truth." She stooped to pick up Albert's little sister, who was still whimpering and hiccuping.

"Mom, I know she's lying. Because I saw . . ." And as he said it, he wasn't sure, after all, of what he had seen.

"Phil." That's all Mom said. But he heard the warning in her voice, and disappointment.

Dad just looked at him.

"But why does she keep talking about it?" he complained.

Everyone turned back to look at Maggie.

"Because I thought of doing it." Maggie threw it at them like a hard, defiant pitch. "Just thought of it. But she tripped all by herself," Maggie said. "Then I really wanted to catch her." As she talked, Maggie tried to keep from crying. But great gulps and heaves forced themselves out of her.

"Don't, don't cry." Meredith leaned over and put her arms around Maggie.

"I'm not," said Maggie between gulps. She pulled herself away. "It's your fault," she said, looking up at Meredith. Her bottom lip was pushed out. Tears were streaming down her face.

"My fault?" said Meredith, flushing.

"If you'd been small . . ." was Maggie's last woeful cry before she pushed past them and ran into the house.

"If I'd been small?" Meredith looked around uncomfortably for an explanation.

"Don't worry, dear," said Mom, patting Meredith's curly head. "I don't understand any better than you do. But we love you exactly as you are."

"Phil," said Dad, "can you enlighten us?"

How easy it was to do. When there was nothing to hide anymore. Of course, Maggie didn't know that or she could have explained better.

Phil told again about the postcards—one and two, about what Maggie had said, about what she had expected. "And I've tried, Mom," he concluded. "She won't do anything with—"

"Me?" said Meredith. "To think I should make such a difference to someone I hardly noticed."

"Maggie has to learn to share Phil," said Dad.

"Wait a minute," said Phil. "Most of the time she doesn't even know I exist."

"Want . . ." Sniffle, sniffle. "Want . . ." Another sniffle. "Maggie." Albert's little sister was struggling to get down.

"Yes, she does, Phil. That's what this is all about." Mom was helping Albert's little sister up the steps. "She'd probably never admit it, but she needs you."

Now everyone was looking at him.

"Well, I won't need her or anybody," he said, "once I get my silver kite."

To Phil's astonishment, Mom, Dad, and Meredith all smiled.

"We've got hold of your string, Phil," said Dad. "We won't let you fly away."

"And look what's happened. Now I have to paint again before I can get it." It was hard for Phil to sound angry at those smiling, affectionate faces.

"It did look nice," said Dad. "But it will look truly professional after a second coat. Just the outside. First thing after lunch. An hour and the job will be done."

"But we had plans, Dad. For the afternoon."

"Not to worry," said Meredith. "I'll fix everything. I'll even get small for Maggie. Bring me the green bottle. I'll climb into it."

{ Guardian of the Kite }

The strange thing was when Phil finished painting on Sunday afternoon, nobody was around, but before he started, everyone seemed interested.

"I've cleaned your brush for you," said Dad. "So you're set to go."

"Are you starting now?" asked Maggie, bouncing up beside him when he left the lunch table.

"Just leave your dishes, Phillie," said Mom. "I'm sure you need to get started."

Even Albert wanted to know how long it was going to take.

"Not too long," said Phil. That was what he hoped.

"Well, how long?" insisted Albert.

"Dad said an hour," admitted Phil.

"I'll set my alarm," said Albert, fiddling with his watch.

"Don't bother." What good would an alarm do? He would be done when he was done.

"Albert," Maggie called from the door, "come on." Then to Phil, prodding him once again: "Are you starting now?"

"Yes. Stop bothering me," grumbled Phil.

And finally, to his immense surprise, Meredith's dad pulled into the driveway, and Meredith flopped out of the car with a little blue backpack over one shoulder. Why the pack?

"Are you just starting?" she asked anxiously.

"Yes," Phil almost shouted at her. "Can't you see?" He pointed to the cellar doors.

"Well, no, I can't," apologized Meredith. "I mean in some places it would be hard to tell."

And that made Phil feel very sorry for himself. If Albert's little sister hadn't sat in the paint, maybe . . .

Meredith was already in the house when he called after her, "What are you doing here anyhow?"

"I came to show you the way to the boat." She stuck her head out the door to answer and then disappeared.

Even Albert's little sister came and stood on the other side of the screen door and said, "Wet. Paint wet."

"That's right." He heard Maggie's voice. "Don't touch."

"Would you take her up for her nap?" Mom called from the kitchen.

"Melodith," said Albert's little sister. "I want Melodith."

"Do you mind if I come, too?" he heard Meredith ask Maggie. He couldn't hear Maggie's answer. But he heard Meredith say, as they were going upstairs, "I'd like to learn what to do."

A second coat certainly covered more quickly than a first coat. The main difficulty was telling where he'd painted and where he hadn't. Phil thought of singing his painting song. But he didn't feel as sure of getting the kite as he had yesterday. Especially not sure of getting it tomorrow. He was becoming cautious now about predicting the future.

Then, after overwhelming him with questions, everybody vanished. He thought he heard Albert and Mom whispering in the kitchen. But when he listened carefully to be certain, there was silence. And just when he was sure he heard giggling and whispering, he decided he didn't hear anything. Or did he hear Maggie saying "sh-h-h-h" in her bossy way? There was the smell of something cooking, he thought, but not the sound of someone busy doing it.

Dad drove off in the car without saying anything to Phil. It wasn't long before he returned. "How's it going?" he called as he hastily carried a brown shopping bag into the house. And that was the last Phil saw of him.

After Phil painted the final stroke, he stood up and looked carefully at the doors to make sure he really was finished. Were there any traces of gray still showing through? None that he could see. Finished! I'm finished! he wanted to shout. But there was no one listening. A lonely quiet surrounded him.

He rinsed his brush in the turpentine, cleaned it on the newspaper as Dad had instructed him, and went into the house. Nobody there. It was exactly what he had feared. While he was working, everyone else was off somewhere having fun.

If it weren't that the car was still in the driveway, he'd think that Meredith had secretly guided them to her father's boat and that's why she'd come early.

What nonsense, Phil told himself. They were most likely all on the beach. Either way, he felt deserted. He would have to comfort himself as best he could. Perhaps peanut butter on an Oreo cookie, one of his favorite snacks, would help.

The kitchen door was closed. This was the final rejection. With a sense of injury, Phil kicked against the door as he opened it.

"Surprise! Surprise!" All those voices shouting, "Surprise!"

Phil sat down on the stool by the kitchen sink to catch his breath. Then he looked around at the smiling faces. Mom and Dad standing by the refrigerator. Maggie and Meredith together by the stove. Maggie without her visor! And Albert looking at his watch with his other arm raised. "Ten, nine, eight . . ."

Everyone joined in the counting. "Seven, six, five, four, three, two, one . . ."

"Blast off!" said Albert.

"That was perfect timing," said Dad.

And then Phil heard an unexpected sound. A bright, capering, captivating sound. It was the sound of Meredith's silver flute. That was what had been in her pack. Meredith played while Maggie passed a platter of cookies. Freshly baked! Peanut butter chocolate chip. A big improvement over Oreos.

"When?" asked Phil.

"While you were working," said Albert. "Twenty minutes for the mixing. And twelve minutes baking. Three batches. That's thirty-six minutes plus twenty . . ."

"Oh," exclaimed Mom, "I forgot. There's a batch still in the oven." She whisked them out. They were just a little brown.

"I smelled them," said Phil. "But I didn't guess . . . Well, I'll be flummoxed," he said, and everyone laughed, Meredith spluttering behind her flute.

Then Dad dished out the ice cream: Oh-Ho-Oreo. So Phil got his Oreo cookies after all. They stood and sat around the kitchen table, having as many of the warm, soft cookies as they wanted. After time off for eating, Meredith played again—jaunty, frolicking music. Celebration music.

"Look," said Maggie, pointing to the doorway, "I forgot about her completely."

Albert's little sister, holding her blanket in one hand, was joyfully bending her knees up and down, up and down, in time to the music.

"Look, Melodith," said Maggie. She said it in a friendly, confident way. "She likes your music."

"Isn't it time?" Albert was looking at his watch. "Isn't it time to go?" It had already been arranged that the boat would anchor long enough for Albert to fish.

"We'll settle accounts when we get back," promised Dad.

"Couldn't we do it now?" asked Phil. It was urgent. This business of celebrating before he got the kite made him nervous. It might be bad luck. He wanted to have the money in his hand as soon as possible.

$16.50. $1.50 more for the second coat. $1.50 to save. Phil was rather pleased about that, now that he had it.

"You did a good job," said Dad as he handed him the money. "A thorough job. That's what counts."

"It's beautiful, Phillie," said Mom, joining them. "Put your money away, and we'll get started." Albert was already sitting in the car.

"Is it dry?" Maggie looked at the cellar doors anxiously.

"Not yet. So stay away, everybody," said Dad. "You wouldn't like to do some more work?" he asked Phil hopefully.

"No," said Phil. "I'll be busy flying my kite."

"Maybe next summer," Dad suggested.

Next summer. That was forever. That was farther away than the horizon, and Phil couldn't think that far.

A ten. A five. And a one. For safety Phil rolled the money up tightly and slid it into the green bottle. No robber would think to look there. And he put the two quarters under a clamshell. Even though Dad was staying behind to baby-sit with Albert's little sister, a robber might sneak past him.

It was thinking of everything that made Phil wake up at dawn the next morning. A pool of red light spilled up from the horizon, staining the early-morning clouds. What was it? "Red in the morning, sailors take warning." Worry number one. It might rain, and Phil wouldn't be able to fly the kite after he got it.

Was there anything else? Mom had promised to go to the

kite store right after breakfast. So that was taken care of. Albert had warned him that he might have trouble getting the money out of the bottle. But Phil had told him to go fishing and forget it. Meredith had gotten the note out, hadn't she?

What else? Something pricked Phil's mind to a state of red alert. It was like unexpectedly stepping on a sharp spine of beach grass. Worry number two. Someone might have already bought the silver kite. Miserable at the thought, Phil closed his eyes. And then he started seeing pictures. The kite man handing the silver kite to someone with short legs, who turned around and smirked at him. No, to someone who had a smiling Dracula mask on. It was like a nightmare.

Phil opened his eyes and closed them and tossed and turned until he woke Albert. Since he was awake, Albert decided to go fishing. So he and Phil got up, and that woke Albert's little sister. And she with her calls for "bletfist" woke Mom and Maggie.

"Let's go," said Phil as soon as breakfast was over. He had to get to the store before the short-legged person with the Dracula mask or someone else whisked the silver kite away from him.

"Not yet," said Mom. She was sounding edgy. "Meredith isn't due to baby-sit until ten o'clock. The store won't be open, anyhow. Oh, yes, Albert's going to be here, too. I hope she'll be all right." Mom was wiping Albert's little sister's face. Phil was certainly glad she wasn't coming along. She'd be ten times more dangerous in a kite store than Maggie.

"I know which kite I'd get," said Maggie.

"They're expensive," said Phil. "You wouldn't have enough money."

"The butterfly one." Maggie ignored him. Now that she wasn't shy with Meredith anymore, she'd gone back to being bossy. She was always too much of something, thought Phil. But soon he would have the silver kite, and it wouldn't matter.

Meredith arrived, carrying the blue pack with her flute. "Maybe it'll keep the kid quiet and I can get some practicing done," she explained.

"Are you coming or staying?" Mom asked Maggie impatiently. Getting up so early had made them all short-tempered.

Maggie paused, torn, then ran and got her visor.

"Are you excited, Phil?" she asked after she got into the front seat of the car. She lifted her chin, trying to see herself in the mirror with the visor on.

Phil, slumped in the back, didn't answer. He didn't know if he was excited or not. He only knew that it was a suffocating day, still and overcast, that even if he got the silver kite, there wouldn't be enough wind to fly it. Or maybe he wouldn't get it at all because at this very moment someone else was buying it. When they got to the store, the bat kite man would say, "I'm sorry, we only had one kite like that."

Through half-closed eyes he watched the familiar scene, the houses, the stores, the railroad tracks, the gasoline station, the long bridge over the inlet. They were almost at the kite store.

Phil let Mom and Maggie go in first. Then, when he

got just inside the door, he turned and looked up. Yes, of course. He'd known it all along. The silver kite was gone.

"Phil," Mom called, "come and describe your kite."

"This is a real-life nightmare," said Phil to himself, moving toward the counter. Framed by the kites, three strange people stared at him: Maggie peering out from under her visor, the bat kite man with black eyebrows raised over his black-rimmed glasses, and his mother nodding at him.

"The silver kite with the red dragon on it," Phil said when he got there. Had his voice made any sound?

"We just sold one of those," the bat kite man said.

"I know," said Phil.

"Really?" The kite man seemed surprised. "We sold the one on display."

"Yes," said Phil desperately, "that was it." How could he end this? Get home. Get away from everyone, from the disappointment.

"Yes, well . . ." The kite man cleared his throat. "Someone wanted it already assembled," he continued. "But . . ." He left the counter and went through the door behind the screen of kites. Nobody moved. Nobody said a word, not even Maggie.

The bat kite man glided back through the door carrying a long, thin package, which he laid on the counter.

"*You* don't mind putting it together," he said to Phil in a tone that assumed that of course, he didn't. Through the plastic wrapping Phil could see the thin sticks and the silver Mylar covering for the kite.

"Does it have a red dragon on it?" Phil asked.

"You'll get your money back if it doesn't," said the man.

Phil started to unzip the pocket in his camper shorts which held the ten- and the five-dollar bills.

"It's fourteen ninety-five," the kite man said, "plus tax and the string."

"I didn't bring enough money," he whispered to his mother. "I've got more at home." Phil was glad, after all, that he'd done the extra work.

"That's good," said Mom. "But Dad and I will pay for the tax and the string."

"Mom . . ." You are the world's best mom—that's how Maggie would say it. But Phil just said, "Thanks a lot, Mom."

"It's nylon string," explained the man, getting a roll out from under the counter. "Strong. You could fly an elephant from it." He put the kite and the string in a long, thin brown bag (made especially for kites, Phil supposed) and handed it to him. "Hold on tightly," he said. "It flies like a bird. Don't lose it."

Outside the store Phil heard the familiar *whiffle, whiffle* sound of kites fluttering. The wind had come up. It often did after a slow start in the morning. But Phil was convinced that the bat kite man had turned it on especially for him.

When they pulled into the driveway, Phil saw Albert sitting on the front steps. "Got it?" he called.

Phil held the package up so he could see. They all went into the house and spread out the kite and the instructions on the living room floor. Then they carefully fitted the frame parts into the Mylar covering.

Meredith played the flute while they put it together.

"This is kite-flying music," she said. And she cast the notes out of the flute in a string of beady ripples—up and down.

"Like a fishing line," said Albert.

"Like eelgrass," said Maggie.

But Phil knew it was the music of the silver kite.

" 'A' goes here," said Phil, "and 'B' goes here."

"No, 'B' goes there," said Albert.

Maggie sat close to Meredith, watching them. She didn't even straighten the Matchbox toys, which Albert's little sister had messed up while they were away.

After the kite was put together, they attached the string. "Let's try it," said Phil, taking a deep breath. Once over the sand dune, they stopped to decide which way the wind was blowing.

"It's coming from the south," said Albert.

"It's blowing north," said Maggie.

"How can you tell?" said Meredith, twirling herself around.

"That's right," said Phil. The wind was coming along the coast, sweeping away the last bits of morning clouds as though they were nothing more than scraps of paper.

Phil walked farther down onto the beach, and then, standing with his back to the wind, he held the kite up above his head toward the north. He held the kite with one hand and held on to the string with the other. Quickly the wind caught the kite and lifted it out of his hand. Phil let the string out slowly, and the kite rose smoothly, higher and higher.

"You don't even have to run with it," said Albert.

Suddenly the kite dived.

"Look out!" cried Maggie.

But it dived only a few feet and then righted itself. As it got higher, it dived farther, but it always climbed back up again. It was like having something alive at the end of the string. "*Whiffle, whiffle,*" it called as it cavorted in the wind. The taut nylon string was sharp against Phil's hand. But he hardly noticed that it hurt as he looked up at the silver Mylar sparkling in the morning sun. The kite was now so high it was hard to identify the red dragon.

"Will it be here next summer when I come back?" asked Meredith.

"If it is, promise you will," said Phil.

"I do. I do," said Meredith. "I'll come to see the green bottle and the silver kite."

"And me."

"Of course you. I wouldn't care about them without you."

After watching for a while longer, Meredith and the others drifted away, each to do a special bit of beachcombing.

"For washed-up fishing lures," said Albert.

"For shell teacups," said Maggie.

"For a note in a bottle," said Meredith.

Phil hardly noticed that they were gone or how long it had been since they left. High in the blue sky, high above the restless blue waves, the kite soared and dipped. Phil didn't mind that he was there alone. He was the silver kite, tumbling and shimmering in the morning sunlight.

But he was also the guardian of the kite. He stooped to pick up a piece of driftwood and wrapped the thin string around it so that it was easier to hold. "I've got you," he said to the kite as he gripped the stick. "You can't escape."

"Got you!" Maggie—the familiar, interfering Maggie—had crawled up from behind and grasped his ankles.

"Maggie," Phil protested, "you surprised me. That was dangerous. I might have let go." But he didn't shake free of her hands. Instead he let her hold on to him while he held on to the silver kite.